Bernard the Brave

A Miss Bianca Story

Bernard the Brave

A Miss Bianca Story

Margery Sharp

Illustrations by Leslie Morrill

A YEARLING BOOK

Published by
Dell Publishing Co., Inc.
1 Dag Hammarskjold Plaza
New York, New York 10017

Yearling® TM 913705, Dell Publishing Co., Inc.

ISBN: 0-440-40305-7

Reprinted by arrangement with Little, Brown and Company
Printed in the United States of America
First Yearling printing—May 1983

CW

Bernard the Brave

1

How It All Began

IT MAY BE remembered that at the end of *Miss Bianca and the Bridesmaid* the author said that was the very last tale of Bernard and Miss Bianca and the Mouse Prisoners' Aid Society, and so it was. *This* story is about Bernard on his own, for surely his unexampled bravery deserves a book to itself.

Bernard had no idea he was going to be so exceptionally brave. It just happened, soon after Miss Bianca told him she was going to be away for three weeks.

They had been sitting together, as they always did between five and seven in the evening, in the little pleasure-ground surrounding Miss Bianca's Porcelain Pagoda. 'Twas a charming spot indeed, with gay flower-beds bordering a Venetian glass fountain, swing seats to sit on, and for recreation a little light seesaw. A few Japanese parasols, of the sort stuck into ices, merely added color, for since the whole desirable property was situated in the Embassy schoolroom, there was never any fear of too much sun or a passing shower. The schoolroom was where the Boy, the Ambassador's son, did his lessons — and how many happy, useful hours had Miss Bianca passed there, sitting on his shoulder to help him with his geography or history or mathematics! Not even his tutor objected to her presence, after the Boy's mother, the Ambassadress, had explained that Miss Bianca was quite a friend of the family! For the Ambassadress knew nothing of Miss Bianca's hair-raising extracurricular activities in connection with the M.P.A.S.:

4

to her Miss Bianca was just an exceptionally intelligent and charming white mouse. — Charming indeed was Miss Bianca, with her silvery fur and huge brown eyes! The eyes of most white mice are pink; Miss Bianca's were the color of topazes, and fringed by long dark lashes. Bernard was never tired of looking at her; beauty always appeals particularly to the plain, and it must be admitted that Bernard himself was plain as a boot, though very powerfully built and with particularly strong, though short and stubby, whiskers. He would have been quite content just to sit there in the garden looking at Miss Bianca all evening; only she had something on her mind.

For not for several weeks now had the Boy done any lessons. He'd had mumps with complications, and the very next day was to be taken to convalesce in the bracing air of a winter resort in the mountains, and it was this news Miss Bianca had to break.

"My dear Bernard," said she, interrupting the companionable silence, "you know the Boy is well on the road to recovery?"

"Good-oh," said Bernard. "I remember you telling me he had mumps."

"And is now to be taken," continued Miss Bianca, "to convalesce in the bracing air of a mountain resort."

"Very sensible," said Bernard. "One of my nephews — would it be young Nibbler? — didn't properly get over the mumps before catching measles." (No wonder he couldn't remember the name; he had seventy nephews and nieces.) "How long is the Boy going for?"

"Three weeks," said Miss Bianca, "and I'm very much afraid, dear Bernard, that I shall be away for the same length of time. We leave to-morrow morning."

It was a few moments before this information sank in to Bernard's then agitated breast.

"Away for three *weeks?*" he exclaimed. "Why, Miss Bianca, that's ages and ages!" (So three weeks were, to a mouse.) "Why on earth must you go as well?"

"The Boy happens to be rather attached to me," said Miss Bianca modestly.

"As well he may," snorted Bernard, "but he'll have all that bracing air to console him. What about me, left behind with no more than a whiff from the cheese-factory? I shall come too," declared Bernard. "I know *you* always travel in the Boy's pocket, but if I have to hitch-hike I'll make it. I've never seen a mountain," he added. "We could look at one together, Miss Bianca!"

6

Miss Bianca sighed. Fond as she was of her old comrade, and thoroughly as she appreciated his sterling qualities, she felt she was going to have her hands quite full enough without looking at mountains with Bernard.

"Actually I'd relied on your watering my garden for me," said she.

Though it was November, owing to the practically hothouse house conditions in the schoolroom, Miss Bianca's flowers bloomed all the year round, but of course needed a great deal of watering.

"Albert Footman will see to that," said Bernard.

"Actually, since Albert Footman has been courting one of the chambermaids," said Miss Bianca, for once rather censoriously, "he's little better than a broken reed. — My poor daisies! There's a little pink one just coming out."

Bernard paused a moment. Then —

"You mean you'd rather I stayed behind to water your daisies?" he asked.

"To be frank, yes," said Miss Bianca. " 'Twould be the greatest comfort to me!"

Since anything that would be a comfort to Miss Bianca was okay with Bernard, he, however reluctantly, gave up his plans to hitch-hike and promised to stay behind on the job.

He little guessed that when Miss Bianca came back her garden would be dry as a bone!

Next morning off the big Rolls Royce rolled bearing the Boy and his mother to their mountain resort. (The Ambassador couldn't go with them owing to his ambassadorial duties.) The Ambassadress saw her son slip Miss Bianca into his pocket, but only smiled. As has been said, she was very fond of Miss Bianca herself — it was she who'd given Miss Bianca the silver chain she always wore round her neck — and also realized that to be parted from his best friend might well set back the Boy's convalescence. However, since the Boy's pocket already contained two fish-hooks and a lump of toffee, Miss Bianca was out again as soon as in, and he had to turn his pocket quite out before she could travel in reasonable comfort. Then off the car rolled bearing the Boy and his mother and Miss Bianca to the bracing airs of the mountain resort, leaving Bernard behind.

He couldn't even wave good-bye. There were too many footmen about, helping put the luggage in. The car rolled off, and Bernard was left alone.

"It's only for three weeks," he told himself bravely. "I'll have time to get my stamp album in proper order. . . ."

It was only for three weeks. The mornings were all right: first he went and watered the Pagoda garden, also cleaned out (turning the tap off first) the Venetian glass fountain. Then there was all the M.P.A.S. correspondence to see to — for he was still its Secretary, though Miss Bianca had long retired from being its Madam Chairwoman — and after lunch his stamp album to occupy him. But between five and seven he simply didn't know what to do with himself.

Some of his neighbors in the cigar-cabinet where he had a flat invited him to wine-and-cheese parties. — Since the Ambassador stopped smoking, his cigar-cabinet was one of the best mouse addresses going; one of Bernard's neighbors was a fashionable doctor, one a fashionable optician, one a Chartered Accountant; wine-and-cheese parties were part of their way of life, there was one almost every evening. But Bernard soon found them if anything a bore — the conversation so regularly turned on the wonderful adventures he'd shared with Miss Bianca. Not that the *object* of these adventures, the rescuing of prisoners, much interested such sophisticated, worldling mice; to their discredit, none was even a member of the M.P.A.S.; they just wanted to hear about the celebrated Miss Bianca!

"Tell us more about Miss Bianca in the Black Castle!" begged Bernard's neighbors. "How wonderfully brave she must have been, to face that terrible cat!"

"Actually it was me he had actually in his clutches," said Bernard.

"Really? — But tell us about Miss Bianca in the Diamond Palace!" pressed Bernard's neighbors. "Wasn't it quite heroic of her to face those mechanical ladies-in-waiting?"

"Actually it was me, disguised as a knife-grinder, who finally pulled off the rescue," said Bernard — but no one seemed to want to hear about *his* heroism at all!

Thus a rather sore and unhappy mouse was Bernard ere Miss Bianca had been gone but a week. Stumping gloomily back into his own flat after a wine-and-cheese party he slammed the door and put "Out" on it and resolved not to open it again (except of course for the laundry and milk and to go and water Miss Bianca's garden), and lead a hermit's life until she came back.

As the first step towards becoming a hermit he went straight to bed, and having rather drowned his sorrows at the wine part of the wine-and-cheese party, went straight to sleep. How long he slept he didn't know, but it must have been in the

small hours of the morning that he was aroused
by a loud, repeated knocking on his with-"Out"-
on-it front door.

"Botheration!" thought Bernard. "Whoever it
is can just go *on* knocking!"

But it was more than a knocking, it was a positive battering — enough to wake all the neighbors.
Also it didn't stop.

"At least I'll give whoever it is a piece of my
mind!" thought Bernard, as he got grumpily out
of bed and opened up.

There on the threshold stood a mouse so aged
and decrepit (actually on crutches), so apparently
incapable of kicking up such a row on his own,
Bernard instinctively looked past him to see if
there wasn't a gang of young Halloween rowdies

with him. But no; he was alone; and Bernard realized that what he'd been banging on the door with must have been a crutch, used practically as a battering-ram.

"You've been long enough answering," complained the old mouse, "when there isn't a moment to lose! You *are* Bernard?"

"If you mean, am I the Permanent Secretary of the M.P.A.S.," answered Bernard stiffly, "I am. And I think you might have better manners than to come banging on my door when you see 'Out' on it. However, since you seem to know my name, what can I do for you?"

"I don't suppose *you* can do anything," said the old mouse. "Lead me to Miss Bianca!"

"I'm afraid she's away," said Bernard, more stiffly still, "enjoying the bracing air of a mountain resort."

"Away? How long for?" panted the old mouse.

"Three weeks," said Bernard. "Actually, now, two weeks minus a day."

"Then it may be too late!" cried the old mouse; and stumbling in before Bernard could stop him, he collapsed into Bernard's best armchair with his crutches on the floor beside it.

"Well, as you're here, I suppose you may as well get whatever it is off your chest," said Bernard resignedly.

2

Nicodemus' ·Tale

"MY NAME," OPENED the old mouse, now more calmly, "is Nicodemus; nor have I always been as you now see me."

"Well, I should hope not," said Bernard, "because to me, if I may say so, you look a perfect wreck."

"Believe it or not, in my youth I was a Waltzing Mouse," said Nicodemus, "excelling above all in the Viennese variety. It was for that particular skill my young mistress induced her guardian — for she was left orphaned at an early age — to purchase me off an itinerant showman. Ah me, what a happy life I then led, performing not for

ignorant rustics but for a young lady with a
thorough knowledge of music! Naturally time
passed; I grew older; I grew even arthritic; but
did my dear Miss Tomasina ever chide me? No.
She made me these crutches with her own hands!"

"Not a bad job of work," said Bernard, survey-
ing them rather critically, "though I dare say any
one of our joiners would have done better. If you
want her name inscribed in the M.P.A.S. Records
Book, I assure you I can see to it just as well as
Miss Bianca."

"But only Miss Bianca can *rescue* her!" cried
Nicodemus.

For a moment, in renewed agitation, he started
up from Bernard's best armchair with such sudden feverish energy, Bernard was afraid he was
going to have a fit; and with a soothing (also
firm) hand shoved him back.

"Rescue her who from?" asked Bernard.

"Her guardian would tell you, from bandits,"
said Nicodemus, somewhat controlling himself,
"who seized her while walking in the woods. Her
guardian would tell you 'tis bandits who have
stolen her away — for how else account for her
disappearance? But in my belief 'tis he himself
who has caused her to vanish — on the very eve
of her eighteenth birthday, when she comes of

age, in order to claim all her rich heritage for his own! For unless she's there to claim it herself before the Board of Estates, all falls into his hands!"

Bernard went over to the sideboard and poured out two glasses of elderberry-cordial. Elderberry-cordial always helped to clear his mind, and the laws of hospitality forbade him to drink alone.

"I take it that besides being an orphan she's an heiress?" he checked.

"To lands and villages without number!" cried Nicodemus. "To the whole Three Rivers Estate!"

In an instant all Bernard's budding sympathy vanished. The shocking conditions at Three Rivers were notorious even in the city a hundred miles away. Never was a peasantry more downtrodden and abused — compelled to do forced labor, evicted from their homes, their commons stolen away from them!

"The Three Rivers?" he repeated vigorously. "Then I'm not surprised she's disappeared, I'm only surprised she hasn't been lynched!"

"No, no!" cried Nicodemus. "Though the conditions (as you are obviously aware) are deplorable indeed, Miss Tomasina knows nothing of them! Her guardian treats her like a child — and a child she still is — only *nearly* eighteen! When she rides or walks out, 'tis never beyond the Park gates or into the home woods: she sees nothing to displease her eye or arouse her suspicions. *She* has the tenderest heart in the world — didn't she make my crutches with her own hands? — and in my belief 'tis partly for that very reason, because she isn't as cruel and ruthless as himself, and would never be a party to his evil ways, that her wicked guardian has had her made off with!"

Of course this altered the whole complexion of things, and Bernard's sympathies started to revive again.

"I'll tell you how tender-hearted she is!" went on Nicodemus, more and more eagerly. "Once, walking in the home woods, and coming upon a tree-feller who'd had an accident with his axe, she bound up the wound with her own petticoat, which within a week his wife sent back laundered with a bunch of flowers for their dear young lady!"

The recollection was too much for him and he burst into sobs. Great tears started to his eyes and rolled down his shabby whiskers; he wiped them away with his fists — evidently he didn't possess a handkerchief — but still they flowed, while Bernard's sympathies revived more and more. However, he kept a cool head, though in it a daring plan was already beginning to form.

"Well, if she *hasn't* been kidnapped by bandits,"

enquired Bernard, "where do you suppose she is?"

"Why, in the attic of her guardian's town house in this very city!" gulped Nicodemus. "Where else can he be so sure of obedient servants carrying up meals to an imprisoned young lady? — until they perhaps stop carrying up meals at all! Oh, Miss Bianca, how I need you!"

Bernard came to a rapid decision.

"Since Miss Bianca isn't available," said he, "I'll have a shot at rescuing your young lady myself."

Bernard was never in the least jealous of Miss Bianca's fame, but he did for once want to do a rescue off his own bat!

"*You* will?" exclaimed Nicodemus incredulously — yet with rising hope.

"Yes, me," said Bernard. "I've had more experience in prisoner-rescuing than you seem to realize. I don't suppose a few hours will make any difference; you doss down where you are and I'll go back to bed."

For he always believed in getting a good night's rest before any unusual enterprise, and if possible a good breakfast as well.

However, after such a broken night both he and Nicodemus slept most of the next day; and it was rather a high tea (of cheese-parings, bacon-rinds and piccalilli) that they eventually sat down to.

"You said last night," checked Bernard, "that Miss Tomasina is probably incarcerated in her guardian's town house here in the city. What's the exact address?"

"That I can't tell you," said Nicodemus. "All our lives we've lived outside town, a hundred miles off. (If you ask how I got here, it was by way of a farmer's wagon delivering eggs to the General Store.) But what I do know is, it's the biggest house on the Grand Boulevard."

Bernard was impressed. All the houses on the Grand Boulevard were big — one was actually a Young Ladies' Boarding School, and one, when it was torn down, made space for a Supermarket — so the biggest must be a stately edifice indeed, practically a palace, and Bernard had always had a mistrust of palaces ever since his and Miss Bianca's dreadful experiences in the Ranee's palace in the Orient. However, he let none of his misgivings appear.

"Then somehow or other I'll get into it," said he, "and if I find Miss Tomasina there, speak a few reassuring words to her and then — "

"Summon the Police!" cried Nicodemus. "My word, won't they be mad, when they're probably hunting bandits all over the place this very minute! And my word, won't they take it out of her guardian, for setting them on a false trail! Hard labor won't be good enough for him, whilst I personally belabor him with my crutch!"

So saying, he reached for one of the crutches lying beside him and attempted to swing it in the air. — The effort proved too much; his arthritis caught up with him, and he absolutely collapsed with his whiskers in the piccalilli.

"You've done all that could be expected of you already," said Bernard kindly. "You need rest. Just leave the whole operation to me."

For not only did he see Nicodemus, with his crutches and arthritis, as a clog on the enterprise, he also very much wished to pull off a rescue on his own. Putting on his new long-distance glasses, and taking his mackintosh from its peg —

"Leave the whole operation to me!" repeated Bernard, and strode out into the gathering dusk.

3

The Biggest House on the Grand Boulevard

IT WAS JUST as well he'd taken his mackintosh, for the winter evening was cold and drizzly — in fact the drizzle soon turned into a fine but penetrating rain. Bernard was actually rather glad of it, as he turned up his collar and hurried on, for it kept people (and cats) indoors, and he didn't wish to attract notice. The only disadvantage was that the raindrops so blurred his glasses, he had to keep taking them off and wiping them, and even so had but a foggy view of each enormous house. He could tell the Supermarket all right,

from its huge plate glass windows stuffed with breakfast foods and tinned salmon; otherwise, from mouse-level, each house on the Grand Boulevard looked as big as the next. Bernard had to judge simply by the width of their doorsteps; but one doorstep was so unmistakably widest of all, up he confidently nipped.

Then what met his view? The lower panels of a great, shut, oaken door — just like the door of a prison!

"This is where Miss Tomasina is incarcerated all right!" thought Bernard, "but how on earth do I get in?"

His experience of prisons, however, had taught him that however rebarbative their frontage, there was often a weakness at the back; so down he ran again and nosed cautiously round the building's huge bulk, where his expectations were fulfilled by the sight of several overflowing dustbins outside a smaller, more homely entrance. In fact the dustbins so overflowed, the back door was so jammed ajar by cartons and waste-paper, Bernard was easily able to slip in.

First into a cellar, then into a boiler-room. So loudly roared the incinerator in the boiler-room, Bernard skirted it respectfully; and perceived behind it another door ajar, opening onto a narrow staircase.

'Twas a toilsome climb indeed he had to undertake, for the stone steps, though worn, were still steep, and Bernard thought regretfully of the service lifts at the Embassy. "If it's as tough going all the way up to the attics," thought Bernard, "I shall be too breathless to speak even *one* reassuring word to Miss Tomasina!" As the staircase, on the first landing, passed a green baize door on the other side of which (he could tell by the smells) was obviously the kitchen, where there probably *would* be a service lift, Bernard was very much tempted to slip in and chance his luck. But he knew how heavy-handed cooks could be, at the sight of a mouse, and prudently resigned himself to continuing upward toil.

Up toiled Bernard past a second green baize

door, and when he came to a third felt he must surely have reached the attics at last. Pausing only to wipe his spectacles Bernard pushed through it and entered —

Obviously *not* an attic!

It was one of the biggest rooms Bernard had ever seen. It was bigger than the Ambassadress's drawing-room. But a drawing-room it certainly wasn't either. It contained twenty little white beds, neatly ranged in two rows of ten, with beside each a locker or play-box, and upon each a little white nightgown neatly folded. . . .

It took several moments to realize the truth. For the first moment he just thought that Miss Tomasina's wicked guardian must have an exceptionally fine family: families of twenty are nothing to a mouse. Then he recalled that human families are usually limited to five or six at the most, and then of varying ages; twenty little daughters all the *same* age (by the size of their beds and nightgowns) were surely beyond the power of human reproduction. . . .

Also Nicodemus had said nothing of Miss Tomasina's guardian being even married. . . .

At last light dawned: it wasn't Miss Tomasina's guardian's town house he'd penetrated with such pains, but the Boarding School for Young Ladies!

And just as light *did* dawn, in scampered twenty little girls come to tidy themselves up before supper!

To Bernard there seemed at least forty of them, as they ran in giggling and squealing and enjoying a brief interval of release from under the eyes of their teachers. Some were blonde, some brunette, one carroty; some had their hair in pigtails, some in ringlets, some in bangs; but my goodness, how they all giggled and squealed! Bernard's wits were quite bemused, and instead of making for cover he stood where he was obvious to every eye in the middle of the floor.

And did the Young Ladies show any fear of him? Not they. (It may be remembered that Miss Bianca, attacking the Diamond Castle to rescue a little girl called Patience, had based her entire strategy on the hypothesis that the Diamond Duchess's ladies-in-waiting, at first sight of a mouse, would immediately jump on chairs.) But the Young Ladies were made of sterner stuff. (Some of their brothers kept ferrets.) They clustered round Bernard with cries of positive enthusiasm!

"Why, look, here's a mouse!" cried all the little

girls — apparently quite unaware that if they'd had any true feminine sensibility they should have been jumping on chairs. (Actually there weren't any chairs in the dormitory, but they could have jumped on their beds.) "Oh, isn't he cute!" cried all the little girls. "Isn't he cunning?"

They pressed so close, Bernard was absolutely hemmed in by plimsoles; and since in any unusual circumstances it is always best to stick to conventions, he took two steps back, then one forward, and pulled his whiskers.

"Why, look, he's been *trained!*" cried all the little girls. "Oh, isn't he a darling? Isn't he a perfect pet?" (Bernard had never felt such a fool in his life.) "Why, let's *keep* him for a pet!" cried all the little girls excitedly.

"But we aren't allowed pets," said a prim-looking girl in pigtails. "If Headmistress found him —"

"Then she mustn't!" cried Carroty. "Don't be such a spoilsport! *I* know where we'll keep him — in my play-box! It's got holes in the lid where my brother tried out an electric drill and nothing inside but an old teddy bear! We'll put him in my box and feed him cheese from our suppers, and take him out to play with in the dormitory here at night!"

This brilliant plan was at once agreed to, and

26

within moments Bernard found himself popped into one of the big wooden boxes and heard the lid slammed down; and then after hastily tidying themselves all the Young Ladies ran off giggling.

"Here's a pretty kettle of sardine-tails!" thought Bernard grimly.

For though he pushed with all his might, he couldn't raise the heavy wooden lid by so much as a half-inch, and the holes bored by Carroty's brother weren't big enough for even a mouse to squeeze through. . . .

It was true he might have been worse off. At least he wasn't going to suffocate, nor was he likely to starve, if the little girls remembered to bring back enough cheese; but small consolation was either circumstance to Bernard, set out to rescue an imprisoned young lady and now a prisoner himself!

Meanwhile Miss Bianca for her part wasn't finding her hands nearly so full as she'd expected. The mountain resort where the Ambassadress had taken a villa, or chalet, was one of the most beautiful spots imaginable: high snow-covered peaks surrounded a wide smooth lake that reflected the blue of a perpetually cloudless sky, the fir trees,

under their load of melting ice — for the sun,
after each frosty night, shone punctually all day
— looked like Christmas trees; as for the bracing-
ness of the air, it was so remarkably bracing that
the Boy quite recovered almost as soon as he got
there, and had no need of Miss Bianca to keep
him amused!

There was naturally no bathing in the lake, but
there was water-skiing on it, just as there was
proper skiing on the mountain slopes, and the
Boy, as he grew stronger and stronger, began to
take part in both these sports. He also began to
make friends with other children whose parents
had taken chalets round about, and the Ambassadress was pleased to see it, for thoroughly as she
appreciated Miss Bianca's qualities, she sometimes
felt a white mouse not quite adequate as her son's
best friend, and was glad to see him in the company of other boys and girls — as the Boy soon
came to be from the moment he finished breakfast till he was (reluctantly) put to bed.

There were other amusements too, at the mountain resort. Sometimes one of the big hotels put
on a concert, or a fancy-dress dance; once a whole
traveling circus briefly pitched its tents — and
then what excitement! Besides the circus proper
there were all sorts of sideshows; in one an old
lady told fortunes, in another a mustachioed old

man and a lad played on hurdy-gurdies to accompany a pair of Waltzing Mice! The Boy nearly fetched Miss Bianca to see them; then he reflected that the sight might upset her, the poor mice looked so tired!

For of course the Boy didn't actually *neglect* Miss Bianca. As soon as they got to the chalet he made a very nice nest for her in a drawer lined with clean handkerchieves, and never forgot to change them. He also took her for a promenade each morning on the window-sill, brought her up cheese and biscuits after lunch, and before going to sleep always saw that besides his own glass of water by the bed there was a little saucerful for Miss Bianca in case she was thirsty in the night. The Ambassadress kept an eye on her too, and often looked in to report the Boy's progress towards complete recovery. But the fact remained that Miss Bianca was bored stiff.

As usual, she found a resource in poetry — but the poem she wrote after a week at the mountain resort was quite unlike her usual sort of verse!

UNUSUAL POEM WRITTEN BY MISS BIANCA
WHILE STAYING AT A MOUNTAIN RESORT

Without, how white the snow, how blue the sky!
Blue too the lake that ripples to the shore!

All nature smiles! — Alas, ungrateful I
To wish for something more!

Without, the moon in beauty rides on high,
Bright frosty starlets twinkle by the score!
All nature dreams in bliss! — Ungrateful I
To find all nature just one great big bore!
                                                        M.B.

When Miss Bianca reread the poem she tore
it up. But it had undoubtedly been expressive of
her feelings at the time.

Also expressive of her feeling was another,
shorter poem written by Miss Bianca a little later.

SHORTER POEM WRITTEN BY MISS BIANCA

O Bernard, are you quite well?
O Bernard, are you all right?
You will water my garden I know,
I shall find every flower a-blow,
But are you quite well and all right,
Out of my sight?
                                                        M.B.

How Bernard would have rejoiced to read those
simple but heartfelt lines, proving that Miss
Bianca really cared for him!

Of course he was quite *well,* but by no stretch of the imagination could have been called *all right* — imprisoned as he was, at the very moment when Miss Bianca set pen to paper, in a locker in the dormitory of a Young Ladies' Boarding School!

4

Algernon

BERNARD PUSHED AND pushed against the heavy wooden lid until every muscle ached. Then he tried nibbling round an air hole in the hopes of enlarging it sufficiently for him to be able to squeeze through. But the play-box was made of teak, the hardest wood there is, and he soon realized that his teeth would be worn to stumps before he achieved any success. Frustrated and exhausted, Bernard at last quite collapsed — but at least onto something soft. . . .

It was Carroty's teddy bear. As teddy bears go it was quite a small one, little more than eight inches or so long, with gingery fur and boot-button eyes, and a general air of dilapidation only to be expected after a life with Carroty!

"Pardon me," said Bernard — ever polite though practically *in extremis*. "I was so bent on trying to get out I didn't notice you." Then he clutched so to speak at a straw, of which several protruded through the bear's worn gingery coat. "I suppose *you* couldn't shove a bit too?" suggested Bernard.

"Aw'fly sowwy, old chap," lisped the teddy bear (who came originally from a great London toy shop), "but I've lost so much of my stuffing, I'm perfectly incapable of any effort whatever!"

"But this is a matter of urgency," pressed Bernard. "I've absolutely got to get out of here without loss of time in order to rescue a young lady held prisoner by her wicked guardian."

"Goodness me, what an exciting life you must lead!" admired the teddy bear. "You don't play polo too, by any chance?"

"Actually I have," said Bernard. "With an Indian team called the Princely Orchids."

"Dashed sporting chaps, some of those Indians," said the teddy bear. "Dashed good at cwicket too. My name's Algernon, if it's of any intewest."

"Mine's Bernard," said Bernard. "I'm also — if it's of any interest — Secretary of the Mouse

Prisoners' Aid Society; so you'll see why I have to get on with the job."

"You seem to be a dashed sporting chap all wound," complimented Algernon. "All wight, I'll do my feeble best!"

His best wasn't so bad after all; his stuffing wasn't quite all out of him. Bernard's and Algernon's united efforts raised the lid just sufficiently for Bernard to squeeze out — and looking back, he saw that Algernon, by inserting his muzzle (stuffed with wood shavings), had shoved it actually high enough for him to scramble out too.

"I've got so dashed bored here," he explained, "I believe I'll come along with you on your pwisoner wescuing!"

Bernard had first got himself into a Young Ladies' Boarding School, then he'd been called cute. Now the last thing he wanted was an effete soft toy tagging after him.

"Don't think of it," said Bernard hastily. "Much as I appweciate" — Algernon's lisp was catching — "your gallant offer, far better stay where you are!"

But Algernon was already flexing long-disused muscles.

"One of my long-ago ancestors," he remarked, "was I believe spared from being shot by the Amewican Pwesident Teddy Woosevelt — hence our family nickname. How I wish he'd been spared from being shot by George Washington! However, the nickname, as I say, has tagged us ever since, and I must say I'd like to add a little luster to it. Which way do we go now?"

"Obviously first down to street level," said Bernard resignedly — also rather deliberately rolling the *r* in *street* — "to start again; for it seems Miss Tomasina isn't incarcerated here at all. So down again it must be, and I hope you can show me where we get on to the service lift because I've had enough of stairs, up *or* down, to last me a lifetime."

"It's easy to see you know little about boarding schools," said Algernon. "The only service lift *here* wuns non-stop between the kitchen and the Headmistwess's own quarters; all the spoiled paper the Young Ladies have done exercises on in class, like all the Kleenex and curl-papers they leave lying about in the dormitory, are collected in sacks by scwubwomen and taken down to the back door by hand. Actually Addie and Amy should be here in two shakes — which may be a bit of luck for you and me!"

"You mean our best chance of getting down is in a scrubwoman's sack?" demanded Bernard distastefully.

"Our *only* chance," corrected Algernon. "Hark,

here they come! Lie low and pwetend to be dead, like me!"

It was easy enough for Algernon to pretend he was dead. He just *un*flexed his muscles and let himself flop — flat as though he'd been run over. But Bernard was in the pink of condition — (if a little overweight; he weighed an ounce and a half) — moreover, after all his efforts he was still puffing like a miniature steam-engine. However, by lying supine with all four feet in the air he trusted to deceive a scrubwoman's passing glance.

And so he did; for scarcely had Addie and Amy entered and begun their work than the latter let out a squeal quite unlike the pleased squeals of the little girls.

"Goodness, here's a dead mouse!" cried she. "Do put it in *your* sack, dear, for I never could abide mice dead or alive!"

"You're too sensitive for your own good, dear," said Addie, boldly picking up Bernard by the tail and tossing him in among the spoiled exercise papers. "And here's an old teddy bear!" she added. "What rubbish the Young Ladies do turn out of their lockers!"

So in went Algernon beside Bernard; and the two scrubwomen, after collecting all the Kleenexes and curl-papers as well, set off downstairs — chatting all the way.

On the first floor down (against a clatter, through the baize door, of the Young Ladies' knives and forks at supper), they just discussed their Easter bonnets — Easter bonnets meaning as much to a scrubwoman as any topknot worn by a midinette in Paris on St. Catherine's day. But on the second, where the empty classrooms were, Amy thought of something else.

"— with blue velvet ribbons and a pink rose. My goodness, I've just remembered!" she exclaimed.

"That I'm having a pink rose on mine?" said Addie.

"No, dear — though now you mention it, didn't I choose a pink rose first? What I've only just now remembered is that all the dustmen are on strike. So it's no use putting *this* lot outside to be collected, 'twill only mean more mess and litter round the back door!"

"Aren't you the clever one!" admired Addie. "What *shall* we do with them, then?"

"Why, pop 'em into the incinerator!" said Amy.

The ears of Bernard and Algernon both burned and froze!

"Look here —" muttered Bernard.

"Just what I was going to say myself," agreed Algernon.

"We must somehow get out of here before we're, well, burnt to cinders. . . ."

"Obviously," said Algernon. "As to *how,* I leave entirely to you, old chap!"

By now they had reached the cellarage. Nothing now could be heard from above at all — no clatter of knives and forks from the dining-room, no rumor from the kitchen. The only sound that broke the silence was the roaring of the huge, grim, iron-bound incinerator. . . .

But did Bernard fail his companion? No.

Thrusting up through the Kleenexes and curl-
papers, he pushed his head out of the sack and
yelled, "Yah-boo!"

He hadn't yelled "Yah-boo" since the how long
ago Halloweens when but a stripling mouse he'd
followed in his bigger brothers' footsteps demand-
ing tricks or treats!

"Yah-boo!" yelled Bernard again.

"My goodness, it's *alive!*" cried both the scrubwomen together — and (unlike the Young Ladies)
immediately looked about for something to jump
on. — Their only resource was a chopping-block,
left over from the days when the incinerator
burned wood, and on it both huddled precariously
as Bernard finally scrambled out of the sack,
hauling Algernon after him.

"There's a door open behind us," gasped Bernard. "Come quick — Yah-boo! — and we can
get away!"

Algernon followed with for an effete soft toy an
uncommon turn of speed, also with a cry of "Yah-
boo" on his own account, and in two shakes they
were out in the kindly shadow of the dust-bins
while the incinerator, defrauded of its prey,
roared more angrily than ever!

"Well, that danger's past!" panted Bernard.
"I'm still not sure why you wanted to get into

the Young Ladies' Boarding School at all," said Algernon, shaking a curl-paper out of his ear.

"I made a bloomer," said Bernard honestly. "I took it for the biggest house on the Grand Boulevard, which evidently it isn't. It's these dashed long-distance glasses of mine," he added. "I knew at the time I shouldn't have let myself be talked into buying them, and I'll never wear them again! Now we'll just have to *ask* someone which is the biggest. . . ."

At that very moment there scurried into view a respectable-looking mouse who by the size of the basket she carried was taking home laundry.

"Pardon me, ma'am," said Bernard, "but perhaps *you* can tell us which is the biggest house on the Grand Boulevard?"

"Why, the one you've just come out of!" said the washerwoman. "There *was* a bigger — belonging to a gentleman one heard say living in the country — but he sold it to be torn down to make a site for the Supermarket — and I'm sure every mouse should be grateful to him, for the pickings from a Supermarket, after all the lady cashiers have gone home, are a rodent's dream!"

"Thank you very much," said Bernard.

"Not at all," said the washerwoman. "Only glad to be of service. And if ever you should want any clear-starching, the name is Mrs. Nibblecheese."

With that she hurried on; and there was a slight pause, while it began to rain really hard.

"Where do we go now?" asked Algernon.

"Back home," said Bernard, "where I *shall* give Nicodemus a piece of my mind. . . ."

5

A Fresh Start

IT DIDN'T DO anything to assuage Bernard's
wrath that when they arrived at the cigar-cabinet
he found that Nicodemus had got at the elderberry-cordial again. Not only was the bottle Bernard had poured from the night before quite
empty, but Nicodemus had evidently looked into
the sideboard for another, and the level in that
was pretty far down!

"Well?" he cried eagerly, before Bernard had
time to speak. "Have you found her?"

"No," said Bernard, taking off his mackintosh.

"You haven't? Then what on earth have you

been doing, away all this time?" demanded Nicodemus.

"Thanks to you, making a fool of myself," said
Bernard grimly. "By the way, that's Algernon
outside the front door" — though small for a
teddy bear, Algernon was still too big to get into
Bernard's flat — "who has been of the greatest
assistance to me, and who I dare say would like a
little of that elderberry-cordial, as indeed I should
myself."

Just as though it were his own property, Nicodemus tilted the bottle to see how much was left
before pushing it across the table.

"Then all I can say," he snapped, "is that you're
no more good at prisoner-rescuing than my crutch.
Oh Miss Bianca —"

"And all *I* can say," snapped back Bernard, "is
in the first place pipe down about Miss Bianca,
and in the second you're a muddle-headed old
fool." (Here he paused to pass Algernon on the
landing a glass of elderberry-cordial. He also left
the front door ajar so that Algernon could hear
what was going on. He felt the bear deserved it.)
"Miss Tomasina's guardian's town house," he continued, "has been pulled down to make room for
a Supermarket, and the biggest house on the
Grand Boulevard happens to be now," said Ber-

nard bitterly, "a Young Ladies' Boarding School. You seem to know so little about what's been going on, I begin to doubt whether Miss Tomasina has really disappeared at all."

"But she has!" cried Nicodemus. "Indeed, indeed she has! I may have jumped to a wrong conclusion — knowing nothing about her guardian's dealings in real estate — but indeed, indeed she's vanished! One day playing waltzes on the piano, the next totally disappeared — and within but weeks of her birthday! Pray forgive my thoughtless reference to Miss Bianca, and go on undertaking the search yourself!"

"Certainly I shall," said Bernard, "though probably only to find she's visiting friends or relations. . . ."

"But she has no friends or relations!" cried Nicodemus. "Never was a poor rich heiress so alone in all the world! Perhaps 'tis bandits after all who have kidnapped her — but bribed to do so by her wicked guardian!"

"What's your opinion?" asked Bernard of Algernon through the door.

"All bandits being by definition bad hats," replied Algernon judiciously, "and most guardians as well, I'd say it's highly pwobable. Only where do you suppose they've got her?"

"Somewhere in the mountains, of course," said Bernard.

For it was common knowledge that all bandits lived in the mountains, whence they descended to make raids on the peaceful citizenry — and even as he spoke Bernard's heart gave a leap, because anywhere in the mountains he'd be at least *nearer* to Miss Bianca, and might even encounter her at her bracing resort!

"Only don't they cover a goodish awea?" asked Algernon.

"Indeed they do," said Bernard, "and this is where we've got to get some sense out of our friend here. — Now then," he addressed Nicodemus, "where do the Three Rivers your estate's named after flow down from?"

"Why, the great Wolf Wange!" said Nicodemus.

Bernard's heart stopped leaping and thumped. The Wolf Range was the highest, and barrenest, and altogether most fearsome part of the mountains, and it was quite unthinkable that anyone should have built a resort there. Regretfully, he put all thoughts of meeting Miss Bianca aside, and at the same moment remembered something.

"Look here," remembered Bernard, "didn't you say the Police were hunting bandits all over the place already, and how mad they'd be with Miss

Tomasina's guardian for putting them on the wrong track? Now it seems he *didn't* put them on the wrong track; so why haven't they found her?"

"I see you have a better opinion of our Police than is common," said Nicodemus. "I dare say a few might search about the foot-hills, but not one would go up into the Wolf Range!"

("They can't be much like our London Bobbies," put in Algernon. "A London Bobby would go up Alps, in the course of duty!")

"So most probably it *is* into the Wolf Range Miss Tomasina has been kidnapped," said Bernard, "and into the Wolf Range I shall penetrate to-morrow morning. — No you don't," he added, as Nicodemus reached for the cordial bottle again (possibly to drink a toast to Bernard's heroic resolve?). "You just think of anything else useful you can remember, for instance whether Miss Tomasina has anything to recognize her by — such as a mole on the left cheek."

"How extraordinary you should ask!" exclaimed Nicodemus. "Actually she *has* a mole on her cheek — though not on the left, on the right. We used to call it her beauty-spot. . . ."

"At least that's some means of identification," said Bernard. "Algernon," he went on, through the front door, "I shall be leaving to-morrow for the Wolf Range, and how you're to get back to your play-box I'm afraid I don't know."

"I don't either," said Algernon, "but it doesn't matter. I'll sleep here on the stairs and then come along with you. You can't conceive how bored I've been, in that dashed play-box!"

For a moment Bernard hesitated. — It will be appreciated that in this most perilous prisoner-rescuing attempt he hadn't the backing of the M.P.A.S. The M.P.A.S. knew nothing about it, and he didn't mean to let even the Committee know he was going absent. ("The correspondence can just pile up!" thought Bernard.) He was operating entirely on his own, and *wanted* to operate on his own, just to show Miss Bianca he could rescue a prisoner on his own. Nevertheless, the idea of having Algernon for company wasn't disagreeable; and after a moment's hesitation Bernard clasped the bear's paw with grateful warmth.

Immediately, however, there was Nicodemus to be disposed of.

"As my place here'll be shut up for probably several days," said Bernard firmly, "I expect you'll be wanting to be getting back home."

"A hundred miles, on my crutches?" protested Nicodemus reproachfully.

"Well, you got here," pointed out Bernard.

"By means of a wagon bearing produce to the General Store," reminded Nicodemus, "which will have long since returned. Besides, I'm very comfortable where I am: I see you've a very well stocked larder. . . ."

So not only had he nosed into Bernard's sideboard, but into his larder too! — From being merely firm Bernard became absolutely adamant.

"No doubt there'll be some other wagon making the trip to-morrow," snapped he, "which I strongly advise your taking on its return journey. In fact, I insist on your taking it, for mustn't you be there at Three Rivers to welcome Miss Tomasina when I bring her back rescued?"

"But you must bring her back *here*," protested Nicodemus, "out of the clutches of her wicked guardian and to appear before the Board of Estates!"

Obviously he didn't mean to shift; and Bernard stamped out onto the landing to blow off steam to Algernon.

"One thing I do know," he exploded, "I shall put my elderberry-cordial under lock and key! *And* my larder! He can just starve!"

"The old are always selfish," said Algernon philosophically. "How well I wemember my own Gwandmother, after my Dad had been chewed to bits by a Corgi, first bursting into tears and then complaining there wasn't honey for tea!"

"There'll be honey for your breakfast," promised Bernard. "We'll have a good tuck in before we start, while let's hope Nicodemus is still asleep — and when he wakes up won't he get an unpleasant surprise!"

"And serve him wight," agreed Algernon, "for to make fwee with another chap's wine would get him black-balled from any decent club! — By the way," he added thoughtfully, "I suppose you've a plan for getting us *to* the Wolf Wange?"

"I'm just going to make one," said Bernard, who actually hadn't yet given the matter serious thought. "Our best bet of course would be by helicopter, only I don't know when the next one leaves." (Miss Bianca would have known. Ever since her adventure in the Antarctic she always kept an affectionate eye on the helicopter schedules.) "But trust the luck of the mice," said Bernard, "and let me look at a railway time-table."

With which he stumped in again (and would have trod pretty heavily on Nicodemus' toes but that the latter, after so much elderberry-cordial, was already nodding off), and after a short interval returned with whiskers a-cock.

"The very thing!" cried Bernard. "There's a

goods train leaving at six A.M. bound for the foot-
hills of the Wolf Range bearing fodder for the
mountain goats. We'll take it in disguise."

"As what?" asked Algernon.

"Why, as the fodder!" said resourceful Bernard.
"You're stuffed with straw as it is, and where
there's straw isn't there always a mouse too? We'll
have breakfast at five, and then off to the station!
It's going to be a piece of cheese!"

It was a measure of his excitement and resolution that he'd quite forgotten about watering Miss
Bianca's garden!

It wasn't altogether a piece of cheese, however.
On arriving at the station next morning after their
good tuck in (which for Algernon consisted of
brown bread and butter and honey and for Bernard of more cheese-parings, bacon-rinds and
piccalilli, eaten while Nicodemus still snored),
they were first almost drowned by a hose pipe
washing down the platform, then almost trampled
to death by porters not looking where they were
going, then almost squashed for good and all by
one of the big fodder sacks falling off a trolley.
But this last misadventure actually proved fortunate, for as it fell the sack split open at one corner,
and Bernard and Algernon were able to scramble

in among the hay and alfalfa; and unobserved by either guard or driver were loaded onto the train on the first stage of their perilous journey.

No bands played, as on the occasion of Bernard's and Miss Bianca's foray to the salt mines. 'Twas just such an anonymous departure as Bernard had hoped for!

To look ahead a bit, that the rat was let out of the bag was due to that old chatterbox Nicodemus. Some of Bernard's neighbors calling to invite him to yet another wine-and-cheese party found Nicodemus in residence instead; who to

explain his presence immediately told them all about Bernard's heroic bid to rescue Miss Tomasina from bandits. But since the celebrated Miss Bianca wasn't involved, Bernard's frivolous neighbors weren't interested, and considered him merely foolhardy. However, it made an amusing tale, and Bernard being unavailable for their wine-and-cheese parties they invited Nicodemus instead — and didn't he punish the wine, besides taking home enough cheese to keep him going till next evening! Far from starving, he lived on the fat of the land, while the neighbors joked about Bernard's folly. They never thought of alerting the M.P.A.S. — as has been said, not one was even a member — still less of going to his aid themselves. Bernard was just as much on his own (except of course for Algernon) as he'd wanted to be.

To look ahead a bit again, never in the Wolf Range were they to see hair or hide of the Police!

6

In the Wolf Range

THE JOURNEY BY train was uneventful, but on their own indeed felt Bernard and Algernon when it finally halted at that last lonely station in the foot-hills of the Wolf Range, and the sacks were tossed out on the platform, and out from the damaged one they scrambled to survey the grim landscape. . . .

All around stretched miles and miles of first rough heathery grass, then of snow, and there was a slight wind blowing — not a gentle breeze, but a creepy-crawly sort of wind that whined and whistled softly but persistently like the wind through the keyhole of a cupboard with a skeleton

54

in it. No wonder the sacks were simply dumped, for the mountain goats to get at as best they could! "I'll be glad to put into reverse," said the engine-driver. "I've always disliked these parts."

"Me too," said the guard. "I've always felt something unnatural about them. . . ."

"There's nothing unnatural about them at all," said Bernard (bracingly) to Algernon, as the train puffled away. "Everything in nature's naturally natural; the Wolf Range simply happens to be inhabited by ferocious wolves. Besides of course bandits in the higher-up fastnesses where they are holding Miss Tomasina captive, and whither we must now make our way."

"You don't think they might be holding her captive somewhere a bit lower down?" suggested Algernon.

"As to that, naturally we shall enquire of local inhabitants as we proceed," said Bernard, "though in my opinion the higher (from a bandit's point of view), the better. Come on!"

It needed some courage and resolution on both their parts to leave the railway station — their last link with civilization! — and begin the long slog in search of the bandits' lair. All they knew was that they must go *up* — and up how many miles, when to gain but yards across rough grass

was a toil, before they even reached the snow-line! Bernard was nimble, and Algernon dogged, but whether they could have made it is doubtful — and in fact will never be known, since scarcely had they set out when both were bowled head over tip by a whole herd of mountain goats stampeding down to get at the fodder. Algernon, to use his own cricketing parlance, was hit for four, and Bernard would have been hit for a boundary but that he was fortunately (though unwittingly) fielded by the billy-goat; and it says much for Bernard's presence of mind that even as he found himself clinging to a billy-goat's beard, as soon as he got his breath back he took the opportunity to make a first enquiry as to Miss Tomasina's whereabouts.

"There's something in my beard that *talks!*" snorted the billy-goat to his chief wife. (Like all billy-goats, he had several.) "Get it out quick," he snorted, rearing up in terror; "it may be a goblin!"

Like all billy-goats, and indeed goats in general, he was highly superstitious. In olden days goats used to consort with witches, and as a race had never got over the effects of keeping such ill company. It may be said at once there were no goblins in the Wolf Range — just any fluttering broken bit of reed was a goblin to a goat.

"Pray do not be alarmed," said Bernard hastily. "I am no goblin but the Secretary of the M.P.A.S., here to rescue a young lady stolen by bandits; and if you'll only stand still a minute I'll get down by myself."

With which he scrambled down by way of a

long hairy foreleg, and as soon as he reached ground took two steps back then one forward, and pulled his whiskers.

"At least he's got nice manners!" approved the she-goat. "You are too impetuous, my love!"

"It's me who was too impetuous," apologized Bernard, "in seeking news of Miss Tomasina before I'd properly introduced myself. Now that I *have,* you may be of valuable assistance."

"No one who comes impersonating a goblin can expect any assistance from *me,*" snorted the billy-goat, still angrily — for he'd begun to think he'd made a bit of a fool of himself.

"But I didn't," persisted Bernard. "At least not by intention."

"Fur and a long tail!" accused the billy-goat.

"I'm afraid I can't do without either," said Bernard, "but at least I haven't seven-toed feet, which I believe is also the mark of goblins. If you'll just let me recap —"

"Do, my love!" begged the she-goat of her husband.

"— I am here to rescue a missing young lady believed stolen by bandits into the upper fastnesses of these mountains; and you being obviously more familiar with those upper fastnesses than anyone else, perhaps you've seen her?"

"Nary hair nor hide!" declared the billy-goat.

"But I think *I* may have," said his wife. "Didn't I tell you, my love, of the young thing straying out of the bandits' encampment who stroked my coat and called me Nanny?"

"You said it was a boy," reminded her husband.

"So I did," agreed the she-goat. "Perhaps it's *two* poor young things the bandits have captured!"

"All the fodder will be eaten up already," snorted the billy-goat, "if we don't make a move!" — and so saying swept her down with all the rest of his harem towards the sacks still lying on the railway platform. If horns and hooves had clashed before, even more did they clash now!

"Where are you, Algernon?" called Bernard, looking anxiously about for his friend. "Where are you, are you all right?"

"As well as one could expect," replied the bear, painfully picking himself up from a clump of heather, "after being hit for a four. I didn't land as soft as you, old chap: I landed on someone's hoof, and shall pwobably bear the scar on my tum for the west of my life."

"It'll be an honorable one," said Bernard, "and at least we've learned from these harum-scarum animals that Miss Tomasina is indeed somewhere in the upper fastnesses — for that the bandits have disguised her as a boy is more than likely! And I've an idea," he added. "After plundering the sacks, won't they be making *back* into those upper fastnesses, and why shouldn't we hitch a lift? Hang on to a tail, as I will too, and we'll be beyond the snow-line before you can say tin-opener. Are you game?"

"If we both stick together!" said Algernon.

So as soon as the herd started careering back both jumped at the tail of a nanny-goat obviously expecting twins (and who thus wouldn't notice the extra weight), and up both were carried without further effort on their part to well above the snow-line. It was a piece of cheese indeed!

They were actually well above the snow-line

when the billy-goat's chief wife, who had been keeping a benevolent eye on the expectant mother of twins, suggested the latter's taking a rest. "You must look after yourself!" said she kindly. "If you want to rest a moment, I'll wait with you. . . ."

But the expectant mother of twins wouldn't, she was too conceited, and just to show how perfectly fit and well she was, flirted up her tail in such a flourish, Bernard and Algernon were flung off it and on she cantered!

"Never mind," said Bernard, as they picked themselves up. "Just think what miles and miles we've covered! I dare say the bandits' lair is but a couple of steps away!"

Unfortunately, scarcely had they taken the first step when the snow gave way beneath them and they found themselves not in the lair of bandits but in that of a wolf; and though neither parent wolf was at home, what sharp teeth and drooling lips had their four cubs!

7

The Wolf Cubs

THEIR NAMES WERE Red, Rufus, Russet and Ruby (their little sister), and they were waiting for their mother to come back from hunting with their tongues hanging out. As Bernard and Algernon tumbled in between their paws, they squealed with pleasure just like the Young Ladies in the Boarding School — but obviously with no idea of making pets of them!

"Here's at least something to keep us going till Ma gets back!" cried Red. "I don't know what sort of meat the bigger one is, but for my part I'm hungry enough to eat a mouse!"

"It looks quite a *plump* mouse," said Rufus. "We'll eat *it* first!"

(How often Bernard had meant to get his weight down, and now how he wished he *had!*)

"It won't go far amongst the four of us," objected Russet. "I know what! We'll do eeny-meeny-mina-mo, and the one who gets 'he' shall have it!"

"You can count *me* out straight away," put in the kinder-hearted Ruby.

"All the better," said Rufus. "That leaves only three of us. — Red, you're the biggest; you start."

"Eeny-meeny-mina-mo —" began Red.

"Catch a rabbit by the toe —" chimed in Rufus.

"If it hollers, let it go!" chimed in Russet. "One, two, three —"

"And out goes he! It's me!" cried Red, pouncing.

Only just before he pounced, Ruby shot out a paw and scooped Bernard into her own mouth!

"Unfair, unfair!" cried all her brothers. "Just *like* a girl!" they cried. "Put him back into circulation at once!"

But Ruby merely showed her teeth. — She didn't dare do more for fear of actually swallowing Bernard, which was far from her intent (though he, finding himself in a dark red cavern barred with ivory, couldn't know). Meanwhile Algernon, with absolutely heroic self-sacrifice, had thrust his head down between his arms, and drawn up his legs, and was trying to look like a trussed fowl. Actually the wolf cubs had never seen a fowl properly trussed; the snow geese their mother occasionally brought home were all dangling necks and feet; but pretending to be a trussed fowl Algernon looked so much plumper than usual, Red and Rusty and Rufus were ready to have a go at him, and indeed he would have come to a sudden end had not the she-wolf at that moment come home.

She came home in a very bad temper. She had hunted all night long, but unsuccessfully; and besides being very hungry herself, knew her cubs would be bothering her for milk, which she really hadn't got to give them. So she immediately boxed their ears all round, and cuffed their noses for good measure, and declared that she was so worn out she was going straight to sleep and if one of them let out so much as a whimper he'd wish he'd never been born a wolf cub.

"But look, Ma, what we've got!" cried Rufus.

"A bag of straw?" said the she-wolf, sniffing Algernon contemptuously. "You should know better than to try and eat *straw!*"

"Well, Ruby's got a mouse in her mouth," declared Red.

"I never thought to see a daughter of mine descend to vermin," said the she-wolf. "Is this true, Ruby?"

Ruby had just time to cough Bernard up before answering no.

"I'm glad to hear it," said the she-wolf, flipping both Bernard and Algernon out of the lair with one flick of her great paw, "but I'm sure no more troublesome litter of cubs has ever been born!"

Nonetheless, as she curled up in the innermost recesses of the lair, she let Red and Rufus and Rusty and Ruby snuggle in beside her under her brush.

But in what piteous case were Algernon and Bernard — the bear quite muscle-bound from pretending to be a trussed fowl, and Bernard dripping saliva from Ruby's jaws! Despite their more than uncomfortable situation the latter's first impulse was to get himself clean — mice so hate anything sticky or slimy on their coats.

"Get out of that ridiculous lotus-position and help rub me down with snow!" he adjured Algernon. "Is this a time to be practicing Zen?"

"Actually I was impersonating a twussed fowl," said Algernon reproachfully, "in the hope of diverting the wolf cubs' attention. . . ."

"Forgive me," said Bernard. "What heroism, what self-sacrifice, what *imagination!* Can *I* help you get your legs into their usual hanging-down position?"

"Well, a little massage would help," said Algernon.

So Bernard massaged Algernon's lower limbs until he was able to stand upright again, and then Algernon shampooed Bernard with snow until his fur was quite clean again, and both felt much better, and Bernard realized that in considering Algernon no more than a soft toy he'd quite misjudged the bear.

"Never," said Bernard solemnly, "have I met with a stouter-hearted fellow adventurer. Not even Nils, with whom I adventured to the Black Castle, was stouter-hearted! Your name shall be inscribed in the M.P.A.S. Records Book as soon as we get back."

"Thanks aw'fly," said Algernon. "As you know, I'd like a little luster added to it. *Now* where do we go? Not up again, I hope?"

"Certainly not," said Bernard. "We're so far above the snow-line already, I dare say the bandits' lair is so close, only a slight further effort, on the level, will enable us to reach it."

"Couldn't we take a bit of an easy first?" suggested Algernon. (Although as stout-hearted as

Nils, he wasn't quite so active.) "After all that jolting about on goats, and then those wolf cubs, I know *I'm* weady for one!"

So as a matter of fact was Bernard.

"If there was any shelter to be had I'd agree with you," said he. "'Only there isn't."

"Well, what's that over there?" said Algernon.

Bernard looked where the bear was pointing, and saw an old Wellington boot sticking out of the snow like a small, dilapidated, toppling lighthouse. — Who its owner had been, and where the other was, they never discovered; but in fact it was all that was left to tell the tale of a mountaineer who should have known better than to go climbing in Wellies anyway. Now its black rubbery walls afforded a welcome shelter, and within them Algernon and Bernard soon sank into exhausted slumber. They were so tired they slept the clock round and then the clock round again — Algernon dreaming of happy days in London, and Bernard (more gratefully) of the Duke of Wellington.

"Who is this valorous and intrepid mouse I see before me?" said the Duke of Wellington, in Bernard's dream. *"Is it he who routed the French cavalry at Waterloo?"*

(Miss Bianca always did history with the Boy, so Bernard had naturally picked up a bit too.)

"Indeed he is," said the Duke of Wellington's aide-de-camp, *"'by nipping behind all their horses' tails!"*

(This was a memory from Bernard's experiences in the Orient, when he'd played polo for the Princely Orchids.)

"Then introduce him to Queen Victoria at once," said the Duke of Wellington, *"to be knighted for gallantry on the field!"*

"Arise, Sir Bernard," pronounced Queen Victoria, and immediately turned into a Camembert cheese. . . .

It was only a dream, and even in his sleep Bernard suspected it was only a dream, but it was a very agreeable one. He'd have been happy to dream on and on, in the Wellington boot; but when a second dawn dawned he woke up and remembered Miss Tomasina.

"Out we go!" he adjured Algernon, "on the last lap!"

"I'd just dweamed I'd been taken to tea at the Savoy Hotel," yawned Algernon. "What cakes, what ices! But out we'll go if you say so; I feel quite a new bear!"

So off they set in good spirits towards the (they hoped) now quite close bandits' lair where Miss Tomasina (they hoped) was being held captive.

8

Back at the Embassy

WHY THE AMBASSADRESS and her son returned from the mountain resort a week earlier than they'd intended was partly because the Boy seemed completely recovered, and partly because the Ambassador's letters were getting dolefuller and dolefuller. (*"My dearest love,"* he wrote, *"I can't tell you how I miss you, and where are my thick pajamas?"*) Also there had been several thefts from the hotels round about, of fur coats —there were also thefts from the hotels' storerooms, but these the hoteliers could and did keep quiet about — and the Ambassadress certainly didn't want to lose her sables! So as the Boy seemed quite himself again, she decided to return — to the extreme joy of Miss Bianca, who while the Ambassadress packed composed a brief but heartfelt quatrain.

BRIEF BUT HEARTFELT QUATRAIN
COMPOSED BY MISS BIANCA WHILE
THE AMBASSADRESS WAS LOOKING
FOR THE BOY'S ANORAK

Farewell the lake, farewell the snows,
Farewell each sparkling Christmas tree!
How far, far dearer is to me
The humblest flower that in my garden grows!
                              M.B.

But what a sight met her eyes as that evening she re-entered it! All was dry as a bone. The little pink daisy had died absolutely; even the hardiest of her flowers, such as nasturtiums, were drooping on their stalks. Miss Bianca couldn't believe her eyes — she'd so trusted in Bernard to look after them! Immediately, she jumped on the spring of the Venetian glass fountain — but it will be remembered that Bernard had turned it off. "What *can* have happened?" wondered Miss Bianca. Then the thought occurred to her that perhaps Bernard too had been smitten by mumps!

— and without even setting foot over her porcelain threshold, off she hurried to his flat in the
cigar-cabinet, prepared to nurse him if necessary
day and night.

She knocked and rang at the door. There was
no answer. "Is he unable to get out of bed even?"
Miss Bianca asked herself. (Actually it was Nicodemus who wasn't able to get out of bed between
one wine-and-cheese party and the next.) She
knocked and knocked, until several of Bernard's
neighbors came out of their front doors to see
what was going on.

"Why, Miss Bianca, how delightful to have you
back!" cried Bernard's neighbors. "The Boy is
perfectly recovered, we hope? Did you have a
pleasant time at the resort?"

"Yes, no," replied Miss Bianca briefly. "Pray
give me news of Bernard! Is he ill?"

"Ill? Good gracious, no!" cried all Bernard's
neighbors. "Don't you know, Miss Bianca — but
of course you wouldn't, you've been away — he's
gone off on some prisoner-rescuing wild-goose
chase into the Wolf Range!"

And they repeated all Nicodemus had told
them about Bernard's bid to rescue Miss Tomasina
from bandits, just as an amusing tale. But not in
the least amused was Miss Bianca; her whiskers
quivered with apprehension!

"You mean Bernard is in the Wolf Range *alone?*" she exclaimed.

"I believe there's a teddy bear with him," said the Optician — actually he who'd persuaded Bernard to buy his long-distance glasses. "Won't you join me in a glass of sherry, Miss Bianca?"

"In the Wolf Range, among bandits, accompanied by no more than a soft toy!" exclaimed Miss Bianca.

"According to Nicodemus," said the Chartered Accountant. "Actually my wife and I were just going to shake up a cocktail. . . ."

"What *I* believe Miss Bianca would like best is a *tisane*," said the Doctor, "such as *my* wife is brewing this very moment from lime-blossoms. . . ."

For everyone wanted to enjoy the prestige of a visit from the celebrated Miss Bianca!

"How very kind of all of you, but thank you, no," said she. "After so long an absence I have my garden to attend to! — You mentioned a Nicodemus," she added. "Where is *he* to be found?"

"Why, just over the way in Bernard's flat," said the Optician, "where Bernard left him in charge. And no wonder your knocking didn't wake him, Miss Bianca — between one wine-and-cheese party and the next he's dead to the world!"

"Thank you again," said Miss Bianca, with a graceful bow that so obviously preluded her departure, all Bernard's neighbors withdrew into their own flats. But as soon as they *were* withdrawn, once more she rat-tatted on Bernard's door.

By this time Nicodemus was stirring and opened up; and instantly by her ermine fur and the silver chain about her neck recognized Miss Bianca.

"Miss Bianca!" he cried. " 'Tis you at last! Oh that you had returned earlier, for 'tis you alone, I always knew, could rescue my dear young lady!"

With which he repeated in more detail the tale Miss Bianca had already heard from Bernard's neighbors — though omitting his own bloomer in having first dispatched Bernard into a Boarding School for Young Ladies; when Miss Bianca asked how Bernard came to be accompanied by a teddy bear, Nicodemus said merely that the bear happened to be taking the same train.

"And how long have they been gone?" asked Miss Bianca anxiously.

"Four or five days," said Nicodemus. "Time is running out, for Miss Tomasina's birthday, when as I told you she must claim her inheritance, is on the twentieth of this month — so barely a week remains for her to be rescued in! But if only *you* will go after them," begged Nicodemus, "then their efforts may be crowned with success indeed!"

It was now Miss Bianca showed her true greatness of spirit. She *could* have gone after them, by a helicopter she knew bound for a survey of the Wolf Range the very next day. But with a leap of imagination she realized that Bernard 'had gone off on his own because he *wanted* to go off on his own!

"*I* think we may safely leave the whole operation to Bernard," said she, "while I for my part see to my garden!"

Nonetheless, so distressed was Miss Bianca to think of Bernard penetrating the Wolf Range with no stouter companion than a soft toy — she hadn't yet met Algernon, so knew nothing of his straw-filled fiber — she wasn't her usual self at all.

In the Embassy schoolroom life resumed its even tenor; just as usual each morning found Miss Bianca seated on the Boy's shoulder to help him with his arithmetic or geography. But she was so absent-minded, it was often the Boy, not she, who found out an error in addition, or that he'd mistakenly placed the Alps in India instead of Switzerland. In a way it was a good thing, because it meant he had to think for himself more instead of relying on Miss Bianca; but 'twas a very novel sensation for her not to be the corrector herself!

"I hope *you*'re not sickening for mumps?" said the Boy anxiously. "I couldn't bear it if it was me you caught them off!"

Miss Bianca exerted herself to frisk about in a decidedly un-mumpish way. But the Boy knew her too well to be taken in.

"Then something's worrying you," said he, "and I believe I know what it is: you're upset about your garden! I noticed myself it looked all dried up. If the fountain isn't working, I'll soon put *that* right!"

So he did, by merely turning the tap on again; and with jars and jars of water Miss Bianca revived at least her nasturtiums. The little pink daisy, alas, was too far gone. . . .

POEM WRITTEN BY MISS BIANCA
AFTER WATERING HER NASTURTIUMS

Crimson and yellow,
  Amber and gold,
    Striped like a tiger
    On the banks of the Niger,
Was ever a flower
  So hardy and bold?

Without you my garden
Would lose half its charm
But oh my dear Bernard,
I do hope you won't come to harm!
M.B.

It will be seen that the last two lines of this poem had nothing to do with the eight preceding. Miss Bianca recognized the unmatchingness herself, but hadn't been able not to bring Bernard in, she was so worried about him!

The Ambassadress back, and with Christmas approaching, the Embassy was gayer than ever. Folk-dancers danced in the forecourt, string quartets played Mozart in the music-room, in the banquet hall there was a banquet and in the ballroom a ball. The Boy took part in all these festivities with even more than usual enjoyment, but Miss Bianca, instead of attending them all from his pocket — on one occasion hadn't she tripped forth to make her bow to the French Ambassador? — regularly pleaded a headache.

"Poor Miss Bianca! I'm afraid the mountain air didn't do as much for you as it did for my son," said the Ambassadress kindly. "No doubt the altitude was too much for you?"

With a graceful droop of her right-hand whiskers Miss Bianca indicated that the altitude

77

had indeed been too much for her, then with an upward flirt of her left-hand set indicated that she'd soon be all right again, so that the Ambassadress wasn't to worry. Miss Bianca's were the most accomplished whiskers imaginable!

"Then you must just stay quiet and snug in your Porcelain Pagoda," said the Ambassadress kindly.

Snug and quiet indeed could have been Miss Bianca, but for her ever increasing anxiety about Bernard. . . .

"Oh Bernard," cried Miss Bianca mentally, "if only I knew where you *were!*"

It was just as well she didn't know, because —

9

The Avalanche

— BERNARD AND ALGERNON with him were now buried beneath an avalanche.

It had struck, as avalanches usually do, with no more warning than a slight pause in the creepy-crawly wind, only minutes after the pair emerged from the Wellington boot. One moment all was still; the next, with sudden ferocious speed, a great wave of snow crashed down like a demented elephant (only many times larger), and only the fortunate proximity of a clump of edelweiss saved them from immediate extinction. Edelweiss can stand up to anything — it has to — but even the edelweiss crouched almost flat before such an onslaught, and even flatter crouched Bernard and Algernon under its roots. — Instinctively they burrowed farther, into a hollow beyond; and there huddled trembling and for the moment speechless.

"That's torn it!" gasped Bernard at last. "There's no getting out through *that* blockade! Even in the Antarctic I don't remember such a dreadful occurrence! — Oh, my dear friend," he added remorsefully, "to what an icy grave have I led you, for no doubt our corpses will be found, if they ever are, frozen stiff as boards!"

"Yours may be," said Algernon, "but stuffed with straw as I am, I'll be found almost as good as new. But I'll always remember you, old chap; is there anywhere particular you'd like to be buried?"

"Yes," said Bernard. "In some nice, warm, rich, steamy manure."

Where he'd really have liked to be buried was in the Pagoda garden, only he felt it would be too distressing for Miss Bianca to see his tomb every time she watered her flowers. So he said in manure — the thought of which, in his present semi-frozen state, indeed appealed to him almost as much.

"I'll do my best," promised Algernon, "but we're not dead *yet!*"

Bernard pulled himself together.

"You're right," he agreed, more cheerfully, "which considering our experiences with those wolf cubs is a bit of a miracle in itself. We're not dead yet!"

"Excelsior!" murmured the edelweiss approvingly.

"I beg your pardon?" said Bernard.

"I was quoting a poem," explained the edelweiss. " 'A youth who bore, 'mid snow and ice/A banner with the strange device: Excelsior!' "

"Poor chap," said Bernard feelingly.

"Actually it means 'Keep going,' " said the edelweiss. "And since you seem in some difficulty as to getting out the *front* way, why not the *back?*"

"But is there one?" asked Algernon.

"Certainly," said the edelweiss. "Where you are used to be the entrance to a fox's runway, so naturally there's a back door too. Now I really can't talk any more — I'm half choked by snow as it is!"

"Wolves are bad enough, but foxes even worse," said Bernard. "Foxes will eat anything, even vermin." (Being called vermin still rankled.) "However, since it seems our only chance, I suppose we'd better have a shot at the back way — though if we do meet a fox it'll be all up with me at least!"

Algernon this time in the lead, they cautiously explored the back part of the hollow, from which a quite sizable tunnel indeed opened out; they entered it and nosed cautiously on. Overhead the avalanche still crashed with a noise like that of gunfire; but after a little they could hear it no more, and all was still. . . .

The stillness became quite uncanny. Instinctively, they spoke in whispers. . . .

Once or twice they had to skirt the skull of a snow-rabbit, or its hind-leg bones — proof indeed that foxes had used that runway! ("I don't see any skeletons of mice," whispered Algernon encouragingly. "No; *they*'re crunched up bones and all," whispered back Bernard.) However, no fox did they encounter, and for a very good reason which will shortly be disclosed.

And at least, from the gradient of the ground, they were still going up — that is, towards the bandits' lair, not down and so away from it. This had both an advantage and a *dis*; it gave them hope, but made the going all the more toilsome. ("First those stairs in the Young Ladies' Boarding School —!" thought Bernard. "Of all the uphill adventures —!" He was glad indeed not to have Miss Bianca with him; her delicate limbs could never have supported the fatigue. But on Bernard and Algernon plodded. — A plod was rather Algernon's natural gait, except when escaping from an incinerator, but Bernard, like all mice, was used to proceed by short runs, and the enforced slowness of the pace made it all the more wearisome. Also it was now days since either had had anything to eat, and they were absolutely famished.

"Honey, " said Algernon suddenly. "That's what I'd like to get down to — a great big jar of honey. What would *you* like to get down to?"

"Bacon-rinds," said Bernard unhesitatingly. "Though I don't say a bit of cheese would come amiss."

"Nor a slice of brown bread and butter," said Algernon, "just to give the honey body. . . ."

"Sardine-tails . . . ," mused Bernard.

"Cold rice pudding with condensed milk on it . . . ," mused Algernon.

It is common knowledge that the minds of all explorers tend to dwell on food, so Bernard and Algernon weren't particularly greedy exceptions; but what *was* exceptional was that scarcely had each finished describing what he liked best when the tunnel suddenly opened out into a large low cave absolutely crammed with their favorite foods!

Besides the bottles of wine ranged round its rocky walls were sides of bacon, sweet-cured hams, tins of sardines and condensed milk, jars of honey and pots of jam — many of the latter leaking their rich contents into one glorious, many-colored, many-flavored mess. As the Persian poet once remarked (though in rather different circumstances), if there was Paradise on earth, it was here!

So at least felt Bernard and Algernon. For fully half-an-hour they just munched and munched — Algernon switching from honey to jam to condensed milk, while Bernard stuck to bacon. For fully half-an-hour neither uttered a word — their mouths were too full. Then —

"What a perfectly magnificent larder!" admired Algernon. "Whoever do you suppose could have stocked it?"

"Explorers, of course," said Bernard. "I remember seeing just such a cache myself, in the Antarctic. But I must say whoever *these* explorers were, they did themselves jolly well!"

Algernon, his appetite temporarily sated, began to look about a bit.

"Did *your* explorers have hurdy-gurdies with them?" he asked.

"Not that I remember," said Bernard. "Why?"

"There's a couple over in that corner," said Algernon. "You're making a mistake, old man, not to try this condensed milk!"

"First things first," said Bernard, "and the first thing with me is always bacon."

Even on a whole side of bacon Bernard had by now left an impression, for as soon as his first hunger was assuaged he'd nibbled out the initials M. B. on its rind; and was just beginning to nibble a heart round them when Algernon spoke again.

"Well, did they have fur coats with them?"

"Of course," said Bernard. "No one could go exploring the Antarctic without a fur coat. What's on your mind?"

"All *those* fur coats," said Algernon, nodding towards a rack of coat-hangers that almost filled one wall, "look to me as though they'd belonged to ladies. I'm sure one's a mink, and another a sable. . . ."

Now that Bernard took a look too he saw that the fur coats hanging up on the hangers weren't in the least like any an explorer would wear — they were far too fancy!

"D'you know what *I* think?" said Algernon. "I don't believe we're in any explorers' cache at all . . . *I* believe it's the bandits' store-room we're in!"

Which in fact was the case — and glad would the hoteliers at the mountain resort have been to know where their lady visitors' fur coats had disappeared to — let alone all the stores from their store-rooms! Algernon's guess was right: the bandits had moved in (which was why the foxes had moved out), and adapted the cave at the back door of the runway to their own nefarious purposes. They'd shored up the roof, and put shelving round the walls, and slung up racks to hang the stolen fur coats on, and in short made it as complete a robbers' storehouse as could be imagined. They didn't bother to do anything about the front entrance — none of the bandits could have got through it anyway — but entered and exited by way of a cleft under an overhanging rock which Bernard and Algernon hadn't yet discovered.

"By gum!" said Bernard, gazing round in turn. "I believe you're right!"

"Then we can't be all that far from their lair," said Algernon.

"Right again!" agreed Bernard. "I dare say it's quite close. . . . Do you hear anything?"

"Like what?" asked Algernon.

"It sounded to *me*," said Bernard, "like bandit-ish voices uplifted in song."

Both listened intently.

" '*O sole mio*'?" suggested Algernon.

"Something like that," said Bernard, "with a bit of '*Funiculi-funicula*' thrown in. . . ."

In fact it was the sound of song that guided them to the cleft under the overhanging rock. They peered cautiously forth; outside it was now night, but the darkness was partially dispersed by the flames of an enormous bonfire, as well as by the glow from a lesser one serving a culinary purpose. For the bandits were holding a barbecue. A stolen goat roasted on a spit, wine circulated like water, as with voices uplifted in *"O sole mio," "Funiculi-funicula,"* and other popular airs, the bandits celebrated another year's successful robbing.

10

The Bandits' Barbecue

HOW VILLAINOUS WERE the faces revealed by the firelight! All were heavily mustachioed, some bearded; some were scarred from old knife wounds, others pockmarked by gunpowder; but the teeth of all gleamed white and sharp as the wolf cubs'! The Chief Bandit (for so, by the way he ordered all the rest about, he obviously was), was the most villainous looking of all; in addition to mustachios and beard he wore a patch over one eye, so that almost nothing could be seen of his face *except* his teeth; and what made his appearance even more dreadful, the patch wasn't even a plain black one, but white, with a black cross painted on it. Thus when he was referred to as Cross-eye, it didn't mean he squinted — indeed the glance from his other eye was as bold and piercing as an eagle's!

But at least he had the grace to say grace. As the goat began to be carved up —

"Silence, all!" he commanded. (All the bandits stopped singing and bowed their heads.) "For what we have received, may we be truly thankful!"

"To our heroic leader," murmured all the bandits.

"*Now* if you care to burst into song again —"

"For he's a jolly good fellow," caroled all the bandits,

"For he's a jolly good fellow,

"For he's a jolly good fellow,

"And so say all of us!"

"Very nice," approved Cross-eye. "Now before you all start making pigs of yourselves, I ask you to raise your glasses in a toast to our friend with the hurdy-gurdy, who so cleverly discovered which were the best hotels to rob, and to whom in fact we owe this excellent claret."

'Twas no true traveling showman but a bandit who'd played the hurdy-gurdy in the sideshow at the circus at the mountain resort! (The Boy had actually set eyes on him — and *whom else had he set eyes on?*) As the hurdy-gurdy player rose to his feet and bowed, and all the rest cried, "Hear, hear" —

"Not forgetting his nephew — or should it be niece?" added someone slyly.

The Chief Bandit looked benign, or rather as benign as he could, with one eye concealed by a patch with a cross on it.

"Not forgetting, as you say, his assistant — who after the dull life he or she led with his or her guardian I dare say wouldn't now exchange his or her lot for any number of estates! — Why isn't she or he taking part in our celebrations?"

"He or she said she was too tired," explained the hurdy-gurdy player. "Ever since both my Waltzing Mice dropped down dead, he or she's been complaining of headaches. . . ."

"Then a little gaiety will do him or her nothing but good," decided Cross-eye. "Go and fetch him or her at once!"

Off the hurdy-gurdy player obediently hastened; and Bernard and Algernon, who had of course been listening with all their ears, fairly trembled with excitement at the prospect of at last beholding the missing heiress!

For now they were quite sure Bernard's guess had been right, and the bandits *had* disguised Miss Tomasina as a boy, in order to throw pursuers off the track!

"Now is the time to display all our resource and heroism," breathed Bernard, "to rescue her from under the bandits' very mustachios! Be prepared to do or die!"

"Or if she *is* happier as she is," breathed back Algernon, "couldn't we just pack the whole thing in?"

"You know little of the principles of the M.P.A.S.," breathed Bernard. "A prisoner's to be rescued, like it or not!"

The point however remained academic, for when the hurdy-gurdy player returned dragging Miss Tomasina by the wrist, it was all too apparent that far from being happy she was in the last stages of wretchedness. . . .

Pitiable indeed was the small, slight figure now introduced upon the festive scene. Her hair cut short, in rough goatskin breeches and goatskin cap, so like a starveling boy she looked, Bernard couldn't have been certain she was Miss Tomasina at all, save that as she advanced into the firelight there showed up on her right cheek the very mole Nicodemus had described!

Poor, pitiable Miss Tomasina! The bunch of ribbons in her cap seemed to mock the sadness of the pale, pinched face beneath, with a deep wrinkle between the brows and lips that uncon-

trollably trembled. She looked about at the bonfires as though she scarcely saw them; she had
eyes only for the Chief Bandit; and instinctively
dropped a curtsey. . . .

"Forgetting yourself again!" chided the hurdy-
gurdy player.

Whereupon Miss Tomasina awkwardly bowed
instead and made as though to pull her forelock.
— How many tenants or peasants had pulled their
forelocks to *her*, as she rode about her estates!
Now it was she who pulled hers to the Chief
Bandit!

"I'm sorry," she apologized, in a small, weak
voice. "I didn't know my presence was required.
. . ."

"Certainly it's required," said the Chief Bandit,
still with a benign look. "Now that you are one of
us, rejoicings, as well as perils, should be shared!"

"Only I've such a headache," murmured Miss
Tomasina.

The Chief Bandit now fixed her with his other
eye — or rather with the patch with the cross on
it — and Miss Tomasina stared at it as though
hypnotized.

"Of course if you tell me to I must," she murmured, "stay and join in your rejoicings. . . ."

"You say that willingly and of your own accord?" demanded the Chief Bandit.

"Willingly and of my own accord . . . ," repeated Miss Tomasina.

"And you haven't a headache after all?"

"No, I haven't a headache after all. . . ."

"And there's nothing you'd like better than to join in our merriment?"

"Nothing I'd like better . . . ," echoed Miss Tomasina.

"Well, *we* want no such death's head at our feast," suddenly snarled the Chief Bandit. "I had meant to reward you with a sable coat —"

"But I *have* a sable coat!" interrupted Miss Tomasina. "At least," she added bewilderedly, "I used to have one. . . ."

"Take her away before she remembers too much!" ordered the Chief Bandit, "and give her more of that poppy tea! — Now let each eat his fill!"

All the rest were only too glad to do so, while the hurdy-gurdy player hastily conducted his assistant away from the festive scene; and as they skirted the bonfires and disappeared into the shadows, so did Bernard and Algernon.

It needed some heroism on their part indeed to leave their hiding place in the cleft under the rock; but cleverly they avoided the patches of light thrown by the bonfires, stuck to the shadows, and were almost on the hurdy-gurdy player's heels as he and Miss Tomasina reached a small water-proof shelter (made from stolen mackintoshes), whence the hurdy-gurdy player, instead of brewing more poppy tea for his charge, immediately hurried back to join in the celebrations — which naturally he didn't want to miss, he himself cutting so prominent a figure in them!

As soon as he was out of hearing —

"Miss Tomasina!" whispered Bernard, through a flap in the waterproof tent.

There was no answer. Bernard and Algernon crept in, and beheld Miss Tomasina lying face down on a rough straw pallet, shaken by deep-drawn sobs that racked her whole slender frame. — Many of her tenants had to seek repose on just such pallets, but it is to be hoped none had ever cause to weep so!

"Miss Tomasina!" repeated Bernard, more urgently; and now she looked up.

"Who is it that calls me by my rightful name?" she marveled.

"Me, Bernard," replied Bernard, "come with my friend Algernon to rescue you from being kidnapped!"

"What!" exclaimed the missing heiress. "Have

the Police been sent to look for me at last? — But no," she added disappointedly, "you're only a mouse and a teddy bear!"

Bernard, if not Algernon, was used to this reaction on the part of prisoners.

"I also happen to be," he pointed out, "the Secretary of the M.P.A.S., or Mouse Prisoners' Aid Society, while one of Algernon's ancestors was named after a President of the great American Republic. You may place every confidence in us."

He spoke more bravely than he felt, for at the moment he had no idea how they actually *would* effect Miss Tomasina's rescue. He just trusted in the luck of the mice.

"I beg your pardon," said Miss Tomasina. "Who but I should appreciate the heroism of mice? It was the Waltzing Mice who saved me from complete obliviousness by drinking up half the poppy tea the bandits gave me, and so sank into oblivion themselves!"

"How did you get kidnapped in the first place?" asked Algernon curiously.

"I hardly remember," said Miss Tomasina. "I was walking in my own woods when an old man with a hurdy-gurdy came up and wanted to show me how prettily his mice danced. So I went with him to where their cage was — no farther than

the next clearing! — and then when I'd seen
them he offered me a cup of tea, which I felt I
couldn't refuse, he was so humble and pressing.
Little did I know it was poppy tea, that steals
away all will and memory! For the next thing I
knew," said Miss Tomasina, "I was far, far
from home — and somehow hypnotized by a
cross. . . ."

"If you mean on the Chief Bandit's eye-patch,"
said Algernon, "it's only like the one in noughts-
and-crosses."

But Miss Tomasina shuddered.

"You can't have really looked at it," shuddered
she. "It grows first larger, then smaller, then
shrinks into a little ink spot, then grows larger
again. . . . Whatever he told me to do I knew I'd
have to — even to going out disguised as a boy
with the hurdy-gurdy player and his Waltzing
Mice! I only hope I made their last moments

happy," sighed Miss Tomasina, "by playing their favorite tunes!"

"Everything you tell us promotes our sympathy for you," said Bernard. "Are you quite yourself again now?"

"Indeed I am," said Miss Tomasina, "and place myself entirely in your hands!"

This was a bit of a facer for Bernard, who as has been said had as yet no solid plan for rescuing her; but just at that moment — trust the luck of the mice! — he heard overhead the chipper-chopper flipper-flapper of a helicopter about to land!

11

Up and Away!

IT CAME AS A complete surprise to him, since
unlike Miss Bianca he'd never kept an eye on the
helicopter schedules; but he recognized the sound
from his experience in the Antarctic, and at once
took heart. As indeed he was right to, for the helicopter Pilot, mistaking the bonfires for a flare-
path, landed his machine within a hundred yards
of the bandits' barbecue!

In what disarray all the bandits scattered! They
were courageous enough to rob hotels, or waylay
solitary travelers, but not to face anything out of
their narrow though nefarious experience. Moreover, anyone in uniform was anathema to them,

and as the Pilot with gold braid on his sleeve leaned out, each and all fled — some clutching a last fragment of goat's meat, others a half-empty glass — back and down through the cleft into the safety of their cavern. Even Cross-eye fled!

"Extraordinary," said the Pilot, leaning out. "These certainly aren't regulation flares!"

"They look to me more like bonfires," said his Navigator, leaning out in turn, "probably lit by some of those silly idiots at the hotels. . . ."

"We'll just have to take off again," said the Pilot.

"Not without us!" yelled Bernard.

Bernard dashed so impetuously from the mackintosh tent his whiskers were singed by the bonfires' sparks. So was Algernon's fur singed, as he followed after yelling "Help, HELP, HELP!"

"Curious effect these mountain winds have," said the Pilot. "I had the illusion of someone shouting 'Help!' . . . Well, off we go again!"

But by this time Miss Tomasina had stumbled out after her saviors, and the sound of her desperate voice pierced even above the noise of the helicopter about to take off.

"Stop! Wait!" she cried. "Wait for *me*, Miss Tomasina!"

"Good heavens!" exclaimed the Pilot. "The missing heiress all have been seeking high and low! What extraordinary luck has enabled us to find you here?"

Bernard could have told him it was the luck of the mice, but hadn't a chance to.

"Take us on board at once!" cried Miss Tomasina.

So the Pilot did, stretching out a strong right arm to haul her up, while she in turn hauled up Algernon with Bernard hanging onto him, and in two shakes all were embarked.

"What day is it?" panted Miss Tomasina.

"Wednesday the nineteenth," said the Pilot, "or rather, since it's just past midnight, Thursday the twentieth."

"Then it's my birthday!" cried Miss Tomasina. "I may still be in time!"

As soon as she had explained all the circumstances, and how absolutely vital it was she should appear before the Court of Estates in person, the Pilot threw his schedule to the winds and headed the helicopter back for the city.

"What time does the Court sit?" he asked.

"At ten in the morning," said Miss Tomasina. "Please hurry!"

"We'll make it," said the Pilot, "with a lift

from the landing-ground. But I doubt whether there'll be time for you to go anywhere first. . . ."

"Why should I want to go anywhere first?" asked Miss Tomasina.

"Well, for an heiress to great estates," said the Pilot, "you do look a bit of a ragamuffin!"

It was true. Miss Tomasina hadn't seen herself in a mirror for weeks, and when she now did, in a pocket glass supplied by the Navigator, she cried out in dismay. Under the goatskin cap with its draggled ribbons her short hair hung in tangled elf-locks, and under the elf-locks showed a white, pinched face so begrimed by dirt and tear stains, the identifying beauty-spot was quite invisible. . . .

"Take my handkerchief," said the Pilot, "and I think there's somewhere a bottle of tonic-water; and my Navigator, who's a bit of a dandy, usually carries not only a mirror but a comb."

Though it reeked of Masculine Man Hair Lotion, Miss Tomasina was far from disdaining to use it — and only when her face was fairly clean, and her hair fairly in order, did she suddenly realize she was wearing not only a greasy goatskin cap but greasy goatskin breeches!

"It's a pity we don't carry a Hostess," said the Pilot. "A Hostess would fix you up in no time!"

"Actually though we haven't a Hostess on board, we've a Hostess's overall," said the Navigator diffidently, "that I borrowed to wipe down our windows with. . . ."

"Severe reprimand and loss of pay," said the Pilot. "Is it still fairly clean?"

"I'm sure it's clean enough for *me* to wear!" cried Miss Tomasina, "and please thank the Hostess very much!"

While all this was going on no one took much notice of Bernard and Algernon. In fact no one took any notice of them at all; Miss Tomasina had let go of Algernon (and so of Bernard too), when she reached for the Pilot's handkerchief, and though she thought of thanking the Hostess (who wasn't even there), quite forgot to thank her saviors. However, she still wasn't altogether herself, and no wonder, so Bernard and Algernon bore no grudge, but made themselves as comfortable as they could in and on a box of Kleenex, also the property of the Navigator — Bernard by burrowing into its lower layers while Algernon settled down on top. Their prisoner-rescuing had succeeded indeed, but both were tireder than they had ever been in their lives!

"I'd still like to be there," murmured Algernon, "when the Court of Estates sits!"

"Don't worry," said Bernard. "The Pilot will be there — if you ask me he's a bit sweet on Miss Tomasina already! — and I've had a look at his greatcoat hanging up. In its pockets there'll be ample room for both of us!"

They flew on towards the clear, translucent dawn. Below them the bandits huddled in their cave, below *them* Rufus and Rusty and Ruby and Red curled close to their mother, as up the helicopter soared towards the brightening sky. . . .

Or was there a hint of fog about?

12
Fog!

DAWN HAD SCARCELY dawned before the big chamber in the Parliament building was being cleaned up ready for the Court of Estates to sit — for it was so long since it last sat, all was festooned with cobwebs and deep in dust. Half-a-dozen scrubwomen were employed to sweep, and mop, and polish the windows, and among them Amy and Addie from the Young Ladies' Boarding School.

"My goodness!" said Amy. "It's worse than the Young Ladies' dormitory!"

"At least no mice about!" said Addie.

"No, but spiders," said Amy. "And which are the worst I really don't know!"

"Nasty creepy-crawly things indeed!" agreed Addie. "Touching your Easter bonnet with the pink rose on it, mightn't two think alike?"

"Not if one had the thought first," said Amy.

"See what a whole nest of spiders I've brought down!" exclaimed Addie. "Do sweep it into *your* sack, dear!"

"I've told you, I can't abear spiders any more than mice!" cried Amy. "Sweep it into *yours,* dear — and we'll both have pink roses!"

"And you'll the pair of you have your noses put out of joint," observed a third scrubwoman, overhearing, "when you see me with not only roses but feathers, on *my* Easter bonnet!"

But however preoccupied with millinery all did a very good job, and the chamber where the Court of Estates was to sit was left clean as a new pin.

"I just hope that horrid fog doesn't come creeping in!" said the third scrubwoman. "I felt fog in the air when I got up!"

She should have been hired as a weather forecaster by the Air Ministry. However clear and translucent dawn had dawned, there was undoubtedly fog in the offing. . . .

If the fog was approaching the city, it was already rolling in great waves down from the mountains above the Wolf Range — striking almost as swiftly as an avalanche, and to an aircraft quite as deadly!

"I'm very sorry, Miss Tomasina," said the Pilot, "but I think I'd better ground as soon as I see a flat area to land on."

"No, no!" cried Miss Tomasina. "If you do, we may be too late!"

"I happen to have several thousand pounds' worth of Government property in my charge," pointed out the Pilot.

"My estate shall pay for all!" cried Miss Tomasina.

"Or we may all have our necks broken flying into an outlying spur of the Wolf Range. . . ."

"If I'll take the risk, I'm sure you will too!" cried Miss Tomasina.

"Come on, Sir," said the Navigator. "Take a chance!"

(No one consulted Bernard and Algernon; though in fact both were ready to take a chance too.)

"Very well," said the Pilot, "but it'll be flying blind. . . ."

"I can't say I like this case at all," complained

the Judge of the Court of Estates to his wife, as he finished breakfast and prepared to get into the striped trousers and morning coat he always wore under his robes. "Miss Tomasina having disappeared so very recently — and just before her eighteenth birthday! — I don't like this case at all. . . ."

"You've only to do your duty as laid down by law," consoled his wife. "What bothers *me* — you with your bronchitis! — is all this fog about. You must take a muffler and keep it over your nose."

"And a pretty fool I should look," said the Judge irritably, "under a wig *and* a muffler!"

"My word, that was a near shave!" exclaimed the Pilot.

Through the fog a spur of the Wolf Range had loomed indeed, so close that the rotor was within feet of hitting it. The helicopter bounced and lurched as he struggled at the controls; Miss Tomasina and the Navigator hung on for dear life to whatever strap or girder came to hand, and Algernon was thrown completely off the box of Kleenex. (Bernard, lower down, merely felt — if *merely* is the right word — a sort of earthquake.) But as soon as they were on an even keel again, all Miss Tomasina wanted to know was what time it was.

"Ask the Navigator," snapped the Pilot. "I'm busy!"

"Eight-thirty-three," said the Navigator.

"Then there's still time!" cried Miss Tomasina.

"Look out!" cried the Pilot. "Here we go again!"

For scarcely had he dodged the first when a second spur of the Wolf Range reared up, and having zigzagged once the Pilot had to zigzag again. Fortunately he had uncommonly strong wrists, and the machine was in shipshape order, otherwise all might have had their necks broken indeed. As it was, Algernon bounced back onto the Kleenex box, and Bernard, peering up from its lower recesses, asked him what on earth was going on.

"Fog!" replied Algernon. "Fog's what's going on — but how different from a London fog!" (Rather as a Victorian Englishwoman, witnessing Sarah Bernhardt in the part of Phèdre, had observed how different from their own dear Queen.) "I've never seen such a fog as *this* before!"

"Trust our Pilot," said Bernard.

"Obviously there's nothing else to do," said Algernon, "except pray. Actually I once, when I was shut up in that play-box, made a pretty good prayer. Shall I say it now?"

"I'd like to hear it," said Bernard politely.

Algernon cleared his throat.

"*O Lord of Bears, with golden coat,*
"*And boot-button eyes like stars,*
"*Look down upon all Soft Stuffed Toys,*
"*And keep them in your charge.*"

"It doesn't rhyme," objected Bernard, who had been schooled in verse by Miss Bianca. "*Stars* and *charge* don't rhyme. A short prayer I myself happen to have composed, *does.*"

"I'd like to hear it," said Algernon, with equal politeness; and Bernard cleared his throat in turn. "*O Lord of mice,*
"*Save us from traps, and every other man's device.*"

"Is that all?" asked Algernon.

"At least it rhymes," said Bernard.

"Shall I tell you a prayer I made up," murmured Miss Tomasina to the Navigator — the Pilot was obviously too busy struggling at the controls to listen — "while in captivity amongst the bandits?"

"I'd like to hear it," said the Navigator.

"*O Lord above,*" murmured Miss Tomasina,
"*Pity my plight!*
"*Look down in compassion,*
"*And make everything right!*"

"My prayer, when in a jam," said the Navigator, "goes roughly
"*O Lord of the skies,*
"*Grant us Thy grace,*

"Keep the engines going,
   "And us back to base."

Obviously none of these prayers had any poetic merit, but they were still heartfelt; and as Miss Tomasina and the Navigator and Bernard and Algernon repeated them to themselves, as suddenly as it had descended the fog began to clear.

They might yet be in time!

13

The End

IN A STATELY AND now clean room in the Parliament House the Court of Estates was preparing to sit. It was an impressive sight: on a high dais or platform presided the Judge in scarlet robes and full-bottomed wig (but without a muffler over his nose), with seated on either side of him an Assessor in black robes and lesser wig, like a barrister's. Before them, on the floor of the chamber, was a wide table covered with green baize cloth, known as *Le Table Vert,* piled with title deeds and various other documents relating to the property whose ownership they were about to assess — and which

Miss Tomasina's wicked guardian confidently expected to be assessed *his!*

The back part of the room was open to the public, and was crowded with villagers and tenants — including the woodcutter whose gash Miss Tomasina had bound up with her petticoat — who had come all the way from Three Rivers in the hope, however faint, of seeing those expectations disappointed; for all hated Miss Tomasina's guardian from the bottom of their hearts, for his cruel practices of eviction and forced labor and turning them off their commons. Even Nicodemus was there (for he could get about a good deal better than he'd let on to Bernard), in a really good place under the platform's ledge.

Miss Tomasina's guardian had chosen to appear in deep mourning, with a black-edged handkerchief which he frequently applied to his hypocritical old eyes — as green with greed and envy as the baize table-cloth! If the ploy bamboozled the Judge, it didn't bamboozle the tenants and villagers; as he stepped forward to take the oath, all booed and hissed like the geese on one of the commons he'd stolen from them!

"Silence in court!" ordered the Judge. "Or the court shall be cleared!"

The booing and hissing subsided; Miss Tomasina's guardian, his oath taken, proceeded to express his belief that Miss Tomasina had not only been kidnapped by bandits, but also murdered by them — hence his mourning; then came to the point that as it was in any case her eighteenth birthday, and whether murdered or not she wasn't there to claim her inheritance, all fell rightfully into his hands.

"Certainly he has the law on his side," murmured one of the Assessors.

"I fear he has," said the Judge. "Yet the fact that Miss Tomasina disappeared so very shortly before her eighteenth birthday rather troubles one. — Your ward having been missing scarcely a month," he suggested, now addressing Miss Tomasina's guardian, "might you not wait a little, before claiming her inheritance?"

"No," said Miss Tomasina's guardian. "Is the law the law or isn't it? And is or isn't to-day her eighteenth birthday? It is; and unless she appears in person, all her heritage is legally mine. Unless she appears in person —"

"As I do!" cried Miss Tomasina, entering the court on the arm of the helicopter Pilot.

For within an hour of the fog's clearing he had regained his own landing-ground, and though naturally all were surprised to see him back so soon, when he explained that he had the missing heiress

on board his superiors, instead of reprimanding him with loss of pay, laid on a fast car to take both of them to the Parliament House. But the Pilot had been quite right when he warned Miss Tomasina she wouldn't have time to go anywhere else first!

But even in the crumpled overall of an air hostess and with her hair cut short all the tenants and villagers recognized her at once — and what a scene of enthusiasm greeted her appearance! " 'Tis Miss Tomasina!" cried one and all. " 'Tis Miss Tomasina come back to us! Oh, what have they done to your pretty hair?" cried all the tenants' and villagers' wives. "Oh, the villains, to take all your nice clothes away! But never mind, Miss Tomasina, we all know you for our rightful lady!"

"Silence in court!" cried the Judge. "This changes the whole aspect of the case," he added, aside to an Assessor.

Across the big green table Miss Tomasina's wicked guardian glared at her in fury — but so long as there was that barrier between them there was nothing else he could do. Miss Tomasina still clung rather hard to the Pilot's strong right arm, so that Bernard and Algernon, in his right-hand overcoat pocket, were not only a good deal

THE END

squeezed, but couldn't see a thing; but they could hear all right.

"So you, Miss Tomasina," said the Judge, "appearing here in court on your eighteenth birthday, claim, as you may, all rights to all estates and messuages bequeathed by your parents?"

"I do," said Miss Tomasina boldly.

"Then the law awards them you," judged the Judge, "and the case is closed."

"I protest!" cried Miss Tomasina's guardian. "For how many years have I not protected her interests —"

"By turning us out of our homes and stealing our commons!" jeered all the villagers and tenants. "If she hadn't been the sweetest young lady alive, you'd have made us hate *her* too!"

Miss Tomasina's wicked (now wretched) guardian staggered on his feet, and then in a fit of anger and apoplexy dropped down dead. To do him justice, he hadn't been quite wicked enough to attempt Miss Tomasina's life, but he'd bribed the pretended traveling showman to make off with her among the bandits, which was almost as bad.

"Let someone see the body carried out before we sit again," said the Judge, withdrawing.

Immediately all the tenants and villagers swarmed about Miss Tomasina, saying how thankful they were to have her back, and out from under the ledge hobbled Nicodemus on only one crutch, because he was waving the other in the air.

"What, are *you* here, Nicodemus?" exclaimed Miss Tomasina.

"Certainly I am," said Nicodemus, "and if it hadn't been for me you'd never have been rescued at all, for 'twas I who put your rescuers on the track!"

Which in a way was true, though it left out all Bernard's and Algernon's heroism.

"Then get into my pocket and come home with me to Three Rivers," said Miss Tomasina, "to live on cream cheese for the rest of your life!"

Which pressing invitation would at least get him out of Bernard's flat, and Bernard was so thankful he didn't mind having been as he thought once more forgotten. But Miss Tomasina, now entirely herself again, was a true lady.

"But where are the mouse and teddy bear who really rescued me?" she asked.

"By the feel of it," said the Pilot, who'd just been groping there for a handkerchief, "in my right-hand overcoat pocket. . . ."

He hauled Bernard and Algernon out and set them absolutely on *Le Table Vert,* and Miss Tomasina made them the most gracious speech possible.

"Dear friends," said she, "well I am aware how much I owe you! Nicodemus may have put you on my track —"

"Indeed I did!" squeaked Nicodemus.

"— but 'twas your heroism that made my escape possible, and I thank you from the bottom of my heart. If you too would care to come back with me to Three Rivers, you will be welcome indeed!"

Bernard, on the green baize cloth, took two steps back, then one forward, and pulled his whiskers, while Algernon bowed from where his waist used to be before he ate so much in the bandits' larder.

"Think nothing of it," said Bernard, "it was just a run-of-the-mill Prisoners' Aid operation."

"Hear, hear," said Algernon.

"And in fact, now we're home," said Bernard, "and though we fully appreciate your kind offer, we'd rather stay where we are — eh, Algernon?"

"Hear, hear," repeated the bear.

"Not only heroic," approved the Pilot, "but dashed sensible. Now I'll see *you* home, Miss Tomasina!"

Lovingly he looked into her eyes, lovingly she

looked into his — Bernard and Algernon forgotten again! The Pilot and Miss Tomasina
drifted dreamily out; the Courtroom emptied, and
Bernard and Algernon were left to make the best
way down they could from *Le Table Vert,* and
then out and past the biggest house on the Grand
Boulevard — what memories it evoked in both
their breasts! — back to the Embassy and Miss
Bianca's Porcelain Pagoda.

It may have been noticed that Miss Bianca was
not present at the Court of Estates, even though
she knew all about it and what time it was to sit;
and the reason for this was that she was still completely ignorant of the success of Bernard's prisoner-rescuing operation. So far as Miss Bianca
knew, Bernard was still somewhere in the Wolf
Range and Miss Tomasina as well; and she had
no wish to witness the triumph of the latter's
wicked guardian. Had she known the triumph
was to be Bernard's, nothing would have kept her
from the Court — but as it was Bernard was able
to give her a glorious surprise when he rushed
into the Pagoda garden and told her all his tale.
Miss Bianca's huge brown eyes grew even huger
as she listened with ever increasing admiration.
At the bit about the wolf cubs, and Ruby's com-

passion, a tear stood in each, while at the blood-curdling bit about the bandits and their leader who wore an eye-patch with a cross on it, her whiskers trembled in sympathetic horror. The moment when Bernard recognized Miss Tomasina was thrilling indeed — Miss Bianca thrilled in every limb — and scarcely less so the moment when an aircraft of her own cherished helicopter flight swooped down in final rescue! Other exciting bits, such as their running into fog, Bernard left out, in case she quite fainted from too much emotion.

"So Miss Tomasina has been rescued indeed," recapped Miss Bianca at last, "to appear in person at the Court of Estates and claim her inheritance from her wicked guardian?"

"Certainly she did," said Bernard. "And there'll be no more trouble from *him,* because he's dead as a doornail. — I'm sorry about your garden, Miss Bianca."

"As if *that* mattered!" cried Miss Bianca. "Oh, Bernard, how proud I am of you!"

"It was only a run-of-the-mill rescue," said Bernard modestly, "which since you weren't there I thought I'd better undertake myself. . . ."

"But all alone," exclaimed Miss Bianca, "but for a soft toy!"

"Algernon?" said Bernard. "Why, he proved as stout-hearted a companion as Nils! You haven't met him yet, Miss Bianca, but he's just outside."

Algernon could no more get between the golden palings surrounding Miss Bianca's garden than he'd been able to get into Bernard's flat, but as he now pressed his nose to them Miss Bianca extended a grateful hand and laid it caressingly on his muzzle.

"If it was you Bernard wanted to impress I don't wonder at his reckless resolution," said Algernon. "Really and truly —"

Here the bear suddenly paused, while a light of joy shone in his boot-button eyes.

"Did you hear what I just said?" he demanded excitedly. "Bernard, Miss Bianca, did you hear what I just said? 'Reckless resolution'! 'Really and truly'! — Radishes, rhubarb and raspberries!" pronounced Algernon joyfully. "Ravioli, rice pudding and roly-poly! Somewhere in the Wolf Range I've lost my lisp!"

So he had, though neither he nor Bernard had noticed, and exactly where is uncertain. In any case Bernard offered warm congratulations, adding that he for his part hadn't wanted to impress anyone, it was simply a matter of duty such as any Secretary of the M.P.A.S. would undertake,

and it was Algernon's reckless resolution that deserved praise since he wasn't even a member.

"But where will you go now?" he added anxiously. "Now that I've led you from the peace
and security of a play-box in a Young Ladies'
Boarding School?"

"Why, into the *Boy*'s play-box," said Miss
Bianca. "Or rather, into the extremely commodi-
ous bottom drawer where he keeps all the rest of
his toys he's grown out of. There's at least one
teddy bear there already to keep you company!"

"Does he come from London?" asked Algernon
eagerly.

"Certainly," said Miss Bianca. "He was a gift
from the British Ambassador."

"Then we'll form a Club," said Algernon, "and
call it the St. James's!"

(To look ahead a bit, so they did. It was the
most exclusive club ever known, since Algernon
and the other bear, whose name was Nigel, regularly black-balled any other soft toy who wanted
to join. But each month they held a Ladies' Night,
at which Miss Bianca, escorted by Bernard, was
guest of honor.)

"It's going to be the very place for me," decided
Algernon happily. "Just stroke my nose again,
Miss Bianca, and I believe I'll have a nap till

Bernard can take me round, for I'm really uncommonly exhausted!"

Was it exhaustion indeed, or was it tact, that led him immediately to sink into slumber curled up with his muzzle between his paws outside the Pagoda garden?

"Poor bear, how tired he is!" said Miss Bianca. "And how tired you must be too, my dear, dear Bernard!"

"Just a bit whacked," admitted Bernard. "Did you miss me at all, Miss Bianca, while you were away at that mountain resort?"

"Did I miss you!" exclaimed Miss Bianca. "You were hardly absent from my thoughts! I even wrote a poem about you!"

"Really?" cried Bernard. "Really and truly? Oh Miss Bianca, won't you repeat it to me?"

" 'Twas but a *jeu d'esprit* which I've almost forgotten," said Miss Bianca.

"Can't you remember even a line or two of it?" pressed Bernard.

"Well, the *last* two," said Miss Bianca, "were *O Bernard are you all right/Out of my sight?*"

Bernard drew a deep, happy breath.

"Of course I'm never *all right,* out of your sight," said he, "and I certainly wasn't all right in the Wolf Range among the bandits —"

"I know you haven't told me half," said Miss Bianca, "of the perils you underwent!"

"I'd undergo each and every one of 'em again, and twenty times over," said Bernard, "to earn even a syllable in one of your poems. To me, it's better than being in the M.P.A.S. Records Book."

By the Venetian glass fountain their whiskers slightly yet thrillingly touched. But Miss Bianca was too wise to let the thrilling moment prolong itself.

"And now," she said briskly, "after you've waked up Algernon and introduced him to the bottom drawer, I expect you'll want to go round to your flat and evict that really deplorable Nicodemus!"

Starting from a dream of bliss —

"He's gone already," said Bernard, "in Miss Tomasina's pocket. But I suppose I'd better be there to put the laundry out."

"Is it such a toil to you?" asked Miss Bianca sympathetically.

"Well, a bit of a toil," acknowledged Bernard. "I always seem to forget the whisker-towels until half-a-dozen have to go at once and there's nothing to dry my face on."

Miss Bianca took a rapid decision.

"Dear Bernard," said she, "though we can never be more than best, best friends, why not come and live here in the Porcelain Pagoda, and I'll put your laundry out for you?"

Now it was Bernard who showed wisdom.

"No, Miss Bianca," he said. "If we can never be more than best, best friends, I'll go back to my flat in the cigar-cabinet (which really suits me very well), and just visit you as usual between five and seven every evening!"

Miss Tomasina almost immediately married the helicopter Pilot, who gave up his career in the Air Force to help her look after her estates, which soon became the best and most humanely run of any in the country. — "One thing I'm determined on," declared Miss Tomasina, "is that none of my tenants shall ever pull their forelocks to me again — now that I know what it's like!"

She made in fact a far better proprietress than if she'd never been stolen by bandits, and her husband backed her up. On each anniversary of their wedding day all the villagers and tenants turned out with flags and bouquets — but not one ever pulled his forelock!

END

MS READ-a-thon— a simple way to start youngsters reading

Boys and girls between 6 and 14 can join the MS READ-a-thon and help find a cure for Multiple Sclerosis by reading books. And they get two rewards — the enjoyment of reading, and the great feeling that comes from helping others.

Parents and educators: For complete information call your local MS chapter. Or mail the coupon below.

Kids can help, too!

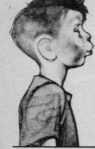

LLOYD ALEXANDER

THE PRYDAIN CHRONICLES

These fantasy classics follow Assistant Pig-Keeper Taran and his companions through many magical adventures in their struggle against the evil Lord of Death. The five-book series is packed with action, humor, and gallantry that will keep readers of all ages coming back for more.

_____THE BOOK OF THREE $2.50 (40702-8)

_____THE BLACK CAULDRON.............$2.25 (40649-8)

_____THE CASTLE OF LLYR.................$2.25 (41125-4)

_____TARAN WANDERER......................$2.75 (48483-9)

_____THE HIGH KING...........................$2.75 (43574-9)

And...revisit Prydain in the six enchanting short stories in:

_____THE FOUNDLING..........................$1.95 (42536-0)

YEARLING BOOKS

PEGGY PARISH

Perplexing mysteries for young people

Amateur sleuths Liza, Bill, and Jed spend each summer vacation with their grandparents on Pirate Island. And each summer brings a mystery more exciting than the last. Whether it's a frightening run-in with the eccentric Hermit Dan or an accident-ridden midnight foray into the woods, the dynamic trio is always stirring up plenty of excitement. Read all about them in: